THE WOLF LOVER'S  GUIDE TO RAISING DOGS

OLIVER STARR

eBook ISBN: 978-1-967106-89-9
Paperback ISBN: 978-1-967106-90-5
Hardcover ISBN: 978-1-967106-91-2

Contents

Bixby "King Wooly," a mentor dog without equal, and the best friend I'll ever have.

Dedication

This book is dedicated to the people, dogs, and wolves who made it possible for me to create this work. First and foremost, I'd like to thank my mom, Jackie Starr, who indulged all my childhood interests, not the least of which was wolves. I'd also like to thank my brother Spencer and his wife Sharon for their unwavering support during some of the most challenging times in my life. My brother Joe for reminding me what courage looks like in the face of nearly insurmountable odds. My brother Ephraim, for being a source of valuable counsel whenever I need it. My wife Thanya, the world's best Wolf-Mom, and the reason I get to spend most of my time in the woods with the wolves. And, of course, to the many dogs and wolves who have shaped my perception of the canid species and educated me on what it means to be a wonderful furry person.

Among them is my first dog, Telly, who could steal a hot pot off the stove and lick it clean. My dynamic duo, Shasta and Juneau, who helped me take the first steps on my wolfy path. Jake, the wolf who ate me. My first true wolf companions Tahoe and Karma. My extraordinary Wooly Malamute Bixby, the best dog I'll ever know and love. My Princess Bitchypants, Aqutaq, the matriarch of our family group and the muse from which all my inspiration is drawn. My current yearlings, Sunny and Moonie, for being a never-ending source of joy in my life. My proper gentleman, Iqniq, the biggest wolf I've ever seen and the nicest one too. Nepenthe, the unruly, Wooly Malamute puppy who's the inspiration for a book in her own right. And finally, my current rescue, Nunarjuaq, who is going to try my patience in all the best ways possible.

My lifelong obsession - 40 years of wolves. Here photographed with Taqqiq "Moonie" and Siqiniq "Sunny," by my sister-in-law, Sharon Montrose.

The book that started my lifelong wolf obsession; "A Wolf of My Own."

Foreword

blame this book on my mother, Jackie Star. When I was four or five years old, she read me a book called *A Wolf of My Own*. It's about a little girl who gets a striped box with holes and hopes it's a wolf. It turns out to be a puppy, but in her imagination, the puppy becomes a wolf. The book captivated me. Unfortunately for me and my mother, I was a literal child. I didn't want a puppy; I wanted a wolf.

I was also a pragmatic little boy and understood that getting a wolf would not be something that resulted in immediate gratification. This desire set me on my lifelong trajectory to study, know, understand, and ultimately cohabitate with the species. As part of the process, I discovered strange old men frequently living in the furthest reaches of Colorado—men typically clad in camo and flannel—who had taken it upon themselves in the mid-70s to ensure that wolves did not go extinct in the lower 48.

I somehow figured out who these people were, and my mother, willingly or unwillingly abetting me in my obsession, drove me around so I could meet these strange people, learn about wolves, and pick up lots of wolf poop. I didn't realize it until many years later, but my mother was driving me around to meet my future self.

I have now lived and worked with wolves for the better part of 40 years. I'm one of the few people whose home is entirely within my wolf habitat. This living arrangement means I have to run a gauntlet of giant paws, quick teeth, and crafty brains to get groceries to the front door.

My experience with wolves—or, as I like to call them, **raw dogs**—has been a lifelong tutelage in what it means to be a dog and what it looks like to be a dog's best companion. As a child, I was lucky that my mother was willing to indulge such a crazy interest. As a grown-up, I'm equally fortunate to have a partner who shares my love of the species and is equally indulgent in my pursuit of greater understanding.

The work it takes to do a good job with wolves is not trivial, but the lessons I've learned will help anyone who reads this book have a much better relationship with the domesticated version of the wild beast. I hope you enjoy my stories, anecdotes, examples, and suggestions and that this book will result in you having the best possible relationship with your canine companions—from unruly puppies to ancient adults.

*For the love of a dog. A melancholy moment here with Nepenthe as we reprise a photo
we took with her predecessor, Bixby, 14 years ago.*

Tahoe Wolf Center
Education - Science - Advocacy

How This Book Benefit Wolves

A Wolf Science and Education Center in Lake Tahoe

One of the reasons I wrote this book was to share my love of wolves and inspire people to understand their dogs and wolves better through my stories and examples. But I have a bigger purpose. The proceeds from this book are intended to fulfill my lifelong dream of opening a world-class wolf science and education center here in the Lake Tahoe Basin.

You can read why this is such an urgent project in the epilogue of this book where I explain why wolves are in terrible peril and what we can do to help them.

Fuzzy Nunarjuaq at five months old and already sporting his winter sweater.

Iqniq surveying his domain in the waning sun.

Introduction

My Wish for This Book

This book is not a dog training book. Instead, this book is about having the best possible relationship with your canine companions.

My dogs are unruly, and I hope your dogs are a little unruly, too. Unruly dogs are healthy and happy, and while it may take more work to coexist with a somewhat unruly dog, allowing your dog to express who they are is incredibly valuable for having the best relationship with your non-human companion.

Over the decades during which I've shared my life with these animals, they have taught me much about parenting, about loyalty, about non-verbal communication, about unwritten rules, about love, devotion, acceptance, and transition. In this book, I will examine the basis for how our dogs be-have. We will explore ways that, with simple changes in what we as humans do, we can be more accommodating of our domestic canid companions so that the lives they share with us will be as enjoyable and interesting for them as those dogs are for each of us.

By the end of this book, I hope you know a lot more about wolves, but more importantly, about the wolf in your living room. I hope that you come to believe, as I do, that dogs should be teammates, not inmates. They should have an equal say in many decisions directly impacting their day-to-day lives.

Canines are far more intelligent than we realize. I guarantee you that even a dog of average intelligence knows far more English than any of us knows of our dog's verbal and nonverbal language. I'm convinced that the wolves and dogs that have shared my life understand so much human language that, for the most part, I talk to them as I would any other family member. And over the many years I've spent with these animals, I've learned they talk back to me in kind.

These are fully autonomous beings with the same broad set of emotions that humans enjoy. They can be angry, embarrassed, sad, bored, afraid, be-reaved, or enamored, just like every one of us. All you have to do to know how they're feeling is learn to pay attention.

Who This Book Is for

First and foremost, it's for your dog. I love dogs more than anything. If this book improves the life of every dog whose owner reads it, I have succeeded beyond my wildest dreams.

But of course, I also wrote this for people! If you have read through the first part of the introduction and are still reading, this book is for you.

If you love dogs and have some in your life, you will likely benefit greatly from this book.

And if you love dogs and have always been fascinated by wolves, you're the person I had in mind when I first put my ideas down in writing.

There are hundreds of millions of companion canines in the United States alone.

Unfortunately, not all of them enjoy the best possible life.

If your dog is lucky, you'll be inspired by what you read in this work.

And if you take the concepts to heart and apply them in your own life, I promise you that your relationship with your canine animals will become decidedly better, no matter how good it is today.

Be warned. You may disagree with some of the things I write in this book. You may find some of my positions extreme or controversial. You might find my somewhat blunt style off-putting at times, especially when coupled with my strong opinions about the best way to do things with canine companions. But know this: my goal is for you to have the happiest dog possible, for that dog to live a long, safe, tragedy-free life, and for you and your dog to have no negative impact on other dogs or their humans, or the wild beings that share this planet with all of us.

Today, my dogs love me more than your dogs love you.

But I promise you that tomorrow if you apply the things I'm sharing, you will have a good chance of your dogs loving you as mine love me.

How to Read This Book

There are a couple of ways you can read this book. The best way is from cover to cover. The book is organized generally along the development path canines follow, from puppyhood to teenage years to adulthood and even old age.

However, if particular chapters spark your interest, either out of general curiosity or because you're trying to solve a specific canine problem, there's no reason why you can't jump ahead or read the book in any order you choose. One chapter does not build on the next in any significant way.

Each chapter is structured first with a behavior we see in wolves. Then, I'll examine how wolf experts work with these animals to leverage our knowledge of their behavior. Finally, I'll impart my "Wolfy Wisdom," which is how you can apply this information in a simple and practical way.

In general, this book looks at underlying behaviors found in wolves. It includes insights from my experience and that of other professional wolf handlers who have successfully worked with wolves for years. In many chapters, I'll share stories from my 40 years of hard-earned Wolfy Wisdom—from some of my greatest insights to my near-fatal mistakes. Then, I'll identify how humans and their domestic canines can leverage that knowledge to improve the daily life experience of the human-canine family group. My recommendations also take great inspiration from the work I and other professional wolf handlers have done to socialize some of the smartest, most challenging, and most independent raw dogs on earth.

~ Oliver the Wolf Guy

Iqniq helps me make my position in life perfectly clear.

Who Am I to Write This Book?

Why I'm Called the Wolf Guy

So, who am I to write this book? I'm a guy who has spent the better part of the last 40 years living with wolves. When I say living with wolves, I'm not talking about living in wolf country in proximity to the species, but rather cohabitating with wolves on an intimate basis, 24 hours a day. My home is wholly within a wolf habitat my wife and I constructed many years ago.

We run a small non-profit, The Tahoe Wolf Center, focused on education and advocacy to help people better understand this maligned species. Wolves, or as I like to call them, raw dogs, since they're the dogs nature honed to perfection, unvarnished by mankind's tinkering, are not the direct progenitor of the dogs in our living room today. But they are directly related to such an extent that understanding the social dynamics and behavior of modern wolves can help inform our understanding of domestic dog behavior and how we can have the most beautiful and dog-appropriate relationship with these furry people.

Always Walking! The author with malamute puppy, Nepenthe, and recent rescue, Nunjuarjaq.

An Unlikely History for a Kid to Love Wolves

As I mentioned in the foreword, my path to acquiring this wolfy knowledge began when I was young. I didn't say that my family, deeply involved in the cattle business in Colorado, was not the ideal start for someone who wanted to learn about wolves. With a cowboy for a grandpa, wolves weren't exactly popular. We weren't warm, touchy-feely people when it came to animals. If a steer had a name, that animal was destined for our freezer.

Nevertheless, my unrelenting interest in wolves and my mother's indulgence in her oldest son set me on a trajectory to becoming the crazy old man on the mountain who lives with wolves. My journey to understand these animals has been fraught with challenges, injuries, and big mistakes that had grave consequences. My knowledge has been hard-won. Dogs are much more forgiving of human error than wolves are, and the consequences of making mistakes with wolves range from injury to losing the animals to losing almost everything.

By the time I was 18, I had enrolled in a biology program at the University of Colorado with the idea that four years or so down the road, I'd become a credentialed wolf biologist. At that time, plans to reintroduce wolves to America's First National Park, Yellowstone were just being formed, and I was obsessively interested in what was happening.

This ambitious undertaking to recover an animal our government had spent a hundred years exterminating was one of the most expensive and controversial wildlife recovery projects in history.[1]

Unfortunately, my big mouth got me into trouble as I voiced deep concerns about specific elements of the plan that required weakening the Endangered Species Act to force the reintroduction through. I wrote about it, talked about it, argued with everyone, and ultimately got myself into hot water.

One of my most respected professors told me I needed a different career. He said, "Everyone involved with wolves in every state agency knew who I was, which wasn't a good thing." I stood by my convictions, though. Unfortunately, the dire consequences of lessening the strength of the Endangered Species Act have manifested over the last ten years, resulting in the wholesale slaughter of thousands of wolves where they should be left alone.

---

[1] https://greateryellowstone.org/yellowstone-wolf-reintroduction

Despite these setbacks in my career plan, I was not deterred. I realized there were more ways to work with wolves than in a government position. I've come to believe that people won't save or love what they don't know or understand and that perhaps the best way for me to support the long-term preservation and recovery of *Canis lupus* was not as a field biologist, but as an educator and wolf conservationist, introducing people to ambassador wolves.

Around this time, I got my first low-content wolfdog, Juneau, as a companion for my first Malamute, Shasta.[2] A few years later, having moved from town to a home in the Boulder Foothills, I rescued a higher-content wolf dog named Reina, who someone had let free in the woods near my home, a common fate for these animals when they prove to be much too difficult for most people to manage. Thus began my real education in how to care for and maintain captive wolves.

Then, in 1992, something amazing happened—a group planning an unlawful reintroduction of wolves to Rocky Mountain National Park was found out. While the idea was sound, and lord knows, Rocky Mountain National Park will benefit when wolves return, without the requisite federal process, what they were contemplating was totally against the law and would have been disastrous for the wolves had they managed to release them.

The group had already imported wolves from Canada and was holding them in a compound along the park's border. When federal authorities discovered this, they raided the compound and seized the animals. Most of those wolves were sent back across the border and released since they had only been in captivity briefly. However, one seven-month-old juvenile named Jake appeared too habituated to people for a wild release.

Colorado Parks and Wildlife contacted my former professor for advice on Jake's future. He suggested me—the crazy student who might be right for taking on Jake—and thus began my legitimate hands-on wolf education.

A few weeks after my former professor gave Colorado Parks and Wildlife my name, I found myself backing my battered pickup truck tail-to-tail with a

---

2   For those of you who are unfamiliar with wolf-dog mixes, I typically class them into several subgroups, with animals having a small but obvious amount of recent wolf ancestry called low-content wolfdogs, those with significant recent wolf ancestry and a strong behavioral and physical resemblance to wolves, mid-content, and finally animals with so much wolf content that they're virtually indistinguishable from their wild relatives, high-content wolfdogs.

vehicle in the familiar light green used by state wildlife agencies. In the back of their truck was a big metal box with holes; inside it, a wolf!

The biologists slid the metal crate across the bed of their truck and eased it into mine. They glanced at one another, then at me, smiled, and one said, "Good luck, kid. You're going to need it."

Jake was an actual wolf out of the wild—unlike any animal I'd had before—and it was with Jake that I first started understanding what a raw dog truly is. Humans have shaped the dogs we have in our living rooms over thousands of years; we've co-evolved remarkably well together. But Jake had none of these attributes.

From my perspective, dogs see their kind-hearted humans as universal remote controls—they learn how to push our buttons just right so good things happen: A longing look at the refrigerator and a well-trained human opens it and treats appear; a gentle paw on an exterior door and an attentive human gets off the sofa granting access to the outside world.

Wolves don't care about remote controls. They solve their problems without looking back at humans for help. If they want something from the humming magic box with the food, they'll pull the refrigerator over and help themselves to the contents. If something on the counter smells delicious, they'll jump up, knock everything down, and eat your dinner before you can react. Dogs look for handouts while wolves seek opportunities — understanding this helps you understand your dog better, too.

Despite lacking knowledge—or maybe because of my naivety—I made remarkable progress with Jake—not only getting him leashed—but also taking him on walks—in cars—and even free-running under the right circumstances, like for photo shoots. Watching a responsive wolf run free then return to you feels magical, but the possibility exists that they won't return, which could be disastrous.

Success made me arrogant, though—and ultimately cost me dearly—as you'll discover later.

Today, I'm executive director at Tahoe Wolf Center—a small non-profit devoted to education, research, and advocacy on behalf of wolves and the wild places they need to survive. My goal, should the book succeed, is to use funds generated to scale this operation into a world-class science and education facility fully open to the public—to continue my mission of teaching the truth about wolves to increase their chances of enjoying a complete recovery across the North American landscape and beyond. In addition to benefiting from this book, I hope you'll join me in my larger mission to improve the fate of wolves and all wild canids.

Here I am with our pup, Iqniq, and his sister Ydun at Mission: WOLF, one of the world's finest wolf sanctuaries and wolf education centers.

MoonieBadger - looking like an angry weasel with her pulled back "airplane ears."

Wolf Mom, Thanya, sharing a moment with Aqutaq and Sunny.

Part 1:

Wolf Development

Chapter 1:

There Are No Alphas

The History of the Alpha Mistake

When you hear the term "alpha," what images come to mind? If you're like most people, you either think of big, strong, aggressive men or animals fighting and killing one another to achieve the top rank among their pack mates.

But what if I told you the entire idea behind the alpha wolf myth and decades of dog training theory was based on a mistake?

In the 1960s, a young wolf biologist named L. David Mech was studying captive wolves at the Brookfield Zoo and Research Facility in Chicago, Illinois. His observations of these captive animals led to a tragic misapprehension that has had grievous consequences for wolves, dogs, and even humans that continue to this day. Dr. Mech's error, one that he has now recanted multiple times, was failing to understand that the behavior of unrelated captive wolves had virtually nothing to do with the behavior of wild wolves.

His mistake led to the alpha wolf theory and the subsequent mistreatment and domination of dogs based on the idea that there is an aggressive pecking order in canine groups, enforced through violence and aggression. As anyone who's up-to-date on modern training theory now understands, canines are incredibly smart and emotionally attuned animals who thrive on positive or R+ training methods.

Unfortunately, this incorrect "alpha theory," popularized by TikTok personalities and even television shows like "The Dog Whisperer," has set canine caretakers up for failure, and the dogs handled in this inappropriate way up for abuse and suffering.

This entire theory is false. Unrelated wolves thrown together by humans had to figure out how to coexist in captivity. The behaviors the researchers witnessed and subsequently recorded represented a response to an unnatural situation.

The problem with this concept, as it relates to dogs, is that it isn't grounded in reality. Wolves, and by extension, dogs, are remarkably collegial animals. As social predators, wolves aren't served by harming or intimidating their family members. Wolves must work together to hunt effectively, defend their territories from other wolves, and raise the next generation. And dogs are typically even more collegial than wolves.

While wolves tend to be actively hostile to unrelated wolves, especially when those wolves are caught trespassing, dogs tend to be more inclined to be sociable. In areas where there are large numbers of feral dogs, injurious fights are relatively rare, and fierce barking without any contact or bloodshed most often resolves disagreements.

*Amazing babysitter. Here, Iqniq lovingly guards Taqqiq "Moonie" and Siqiniq "Sunny."
In spite of his massive size, I never have even one moment of anxiety allowing Iqniq to
supervise the tiny puppies.*

The Truth About Wolf Family Dynamics

In reality, wolf family dynamics are more similar to human family dynamics than perhaps any other species on Earth. We now know that wolf packs are families, and the dominant animals, though sometimes called alphas, are simply the breeding pair, otherwise known as mom and dad. There is no fighting your way to the top of some pecking order. No younger wolf is trying to kill its father so it can breed with its mother. It's as ludicrous as a son trying to kill his father so he can mate with his mom.

In reality, wolf family groups are remarkably collegial, and violent inter-family interactions are rare and generally non-injurious. Actual alpha wolves are benevolent parents, not tyrannical abusers. The unfortunate alpha mistake has created a toxic culture in dog training, and even in the manifestation of Alpha culture, as perpetuated by TikTok stars and social media influencers. This repugnant version of alpha masculinity is no more representative of an alpha wolf than is a blue-dyed teacup poodle in somebody's designer doggie carrier.

I've been fortunate to see how wolves treat their young, and it has been the greatest joy of my life to be a surrogate parent to dozens of wolves over many decades. Fortunately, the idea that threatening behavior or dominance through fear and intimidation is an appropriate means of training any dog is falling by the wayside as a greater understanding of wolves and human-canine dynamics has come to the forefront.

Of all the things I've observed in my more than four decades of pursuing a greater understanding of wolves, the one thing that stands out above all others is their congeniality toward one another. Wolves are among the most socially complex and dependent species on earth, and their obvious emotional ties to their family members are obvious to anyone who has invested even the smallest amount of time in studying and observing this species.

As wolf biologist Gordan Haber said of his lifelong work with wolves:

"When it comes to wolves, it's not about numbers. It's about family. A wolf is a wolf when it's part of an intact, unexploited family group capable of astonishingly beautiful and complex cooperative behaviors and unique traditions. If a family group is left unexploited (that is, not trapped, shot, poisoned, or otherwise killed by humans), it will develop extraordinary traditions for hunting, pup-rearing, and social behaviors that are finely tuned to its precise environment and that are unique to that particular long-lived family group."

These attributes are a far cry from the idea that wolves aggressively pursue status amongst one another and that their behaviors are the blueprint for how humans should interact with dogs.

As you'll learn in this book, nothing could be further from the truth.

Your Dog Is Your Teammate, Not Your Inmate

The world's best dog trainers will tell you that the best and most enduring results occur with behavior shaping and positive reinforcement through rewarding desirable behaviors and ignoring behaviors you don't want—rather than cowing dogs into submission or forcing them to engage in behaviors for fear of repercussions. Lucky for most humans, dogs tend to be very forgiving of our transgressions. Somewhat unfortunately, they'll love even the worst of us who have treated them abysmally.

Wolves are not so accommodating. One of my favorite sayings is that lions may be the king of the beasts, but you don't see wolves in the circus. There's a reason for this. A mistreated wolf does not forgive. They do not forget. When you least expect it, they'll take their revenge.

The last thing you want to do is get on a wolf's bad side and then turn your back a few days later. Losing a chunk of a buttock might be the least of your problems, and getting out of an enclosure alive might even be an unlikely proposition.

If you get nothing else out of this book than this, please take to heart that the best relationship a human can have with a dog is one of gentle leadership by example and even co-equal partnership. Dogs are driven to please us. You just need to show them what you want and reward them for doing those things.

We fail to give the intellects of non-humans enough credit. Canines, in particular, have extraordinary emotional sensitivity to other species. They thrive when they know their human companions are pleased and grow despondent when they sense frustration, anger, or displeasure in their stewards.

While it is possible to elicit behaviors you want through aggressive or aversive training tactics, your animal will be much happier if you do so with patience, love, and collaboration. Unfortunately, many of the world's most famous dog trainers subscribe to the ridiculous idea that aggression and domination are the correct means to train dogs or rectify undesirable behaviors, that humans must be "the alpha" if they want their dogs bent to accommodate our will.

Today, top dog trainers use methods described by the LIMA acronym: Least Invasive, Minimally Aversive. These techniques don't rely on the misguided alpha-wolf theory at all, and I espouse them when I need to train a specific behavior in the animals I work with.

Dog trainers who use the outdated "alpha theory " and rely on strong, aversive measures to subdue and intimidate dogs aren't solving problems or training animals. They're setting a terrible example for people who don't know any better. Worse, they frequently kick behavioral problems down the road so the dog's permanent custodian will end up getting hurt later when the dog has had enough of the abuse.

While nobody's keeping statistics, it is my supposition that the most severe household dog attacks occur because people with a problematic dog saw an abuser get a result, tried to duplicate the abusive tactics, and got themselves eaten.

Many problems are easily avoided by employing kindness, empathy, and patience. And if you have a truly intractable problem, especially one that portends danger, get professional help from a canine behavioral consultant who never engages in aversive conditioning of any kind whatsoever. If you need help, seek out someone certified from any of the following organizations. I've described each of these groups and their general practices below.

1. Association of Professional Dog Trainers (APDT)

- **About:** APDT, one of the largest international professional associations for dog trainers, offers continuing education and resources but does not independently certify trainers.

- **Standards and Training:** Members are encouraged to engage in ongoing education and follow a Code of Ethics. The organization provides professional development through annual conferences, webinars, and workshops.

- **Reputation:** APDT members are generally recognized for their commitment to humane, science-based training. Many trainers list their APDT membership to indicate their dedication to professional standards, though APDT alone is not a standalone certification

2. Certification Council for Professional Dog Trainers (CCP-DT)

♣ **About:** CCPDT is a widely respected certification organization known for its rigorous standards. Its certifications, including Certified Professional Dog Trainer-Knowledge Assessed (CPDT-KA) and Certified Professional Dog Trainer-Knowledge and Skills Assessed (CPDT-KSA), are highly regarded.

♣ **Requirements:**
- **CPDT-KA:** Requires 300 hours of training experience in the last three years, passing an exam covering learning theory, dog training techniques, ethology, and business practices.
- **CPDT-KSA:** In addition to the written knowledge assessment, this certification includes a practical skills assessment that demonstrates hands-on abilities in training.
- **Continuing Education:** Certified trainers must recertify every three years by earning continuing education units (CEUs) or retaking the exam.

♣ **Reputation:** Trainers certified by the CCPDT are considered highly skilled, as certification indicates verified knowledge and experience in training based on humane, science-backed principles.

3. Karen Pryor Academy Certified Training Partner (KPA-CTP)

♣ **About:** KPA, established by positive reinforcement pioneer Karen Pryor, is known for its focus on force-free training and clicker training techniques.

♣ **Certification Process:** Trainers must complete the KPA Professional Dog Trainer Program, a six-month course that combines online study and in-person training.

♣ **Program Components:** The curriculum emphasizes clicker training, shaping behavior, positive reinforcement, and learning theory. Graduates must complete both practical assessments and theoretical exams, showing proficiency in KPA's specific training methods.

🐾 **Reputation:** Clients often seek out KPA-CTPs who are skilled in positive, force-free training. KPA certification is respected for the academy's emphasis on advanced, science-based training methodologies and hands-on experience.

Each of these organizations is reputable within the field of canine behavior and training, so accreditation from APDT, CCPDT, or KPA-CTP indicates a commitment to ethical standards, professional education, and science-based methodologies. Trainers with these certifications are often recognized as among the best prepared to handle a variety of behavioral issues and training needs.

In short, don't think of yourself as the male or female alpha, but rather a patient, doting, kind-hearted, but occasionally firm parent, and you'll be well on the way to being the benevolent leader of your own mixed-species family group.

Bixby Starr at age 13. My teammate and best friend. A mentor dog without equal and the canine who set the stage for our success with all our current animals.

Sunny on the run. Wolf pups play a lot. Here, a baby Sunny tries in vain to outrun babysitter Iqniq.

Dreaming and learning. Sunny (bottom) and Moonie, safe and cozy, surrounded by our scents and sounds.

Chapter 2:

Why Do Puppies Dream?

The "Wolf Pup" trailer – fully equipped to bring two tiny pups home – my "Wolf Ball Run."

The Road Trip of a Lifetime: Wolf Ball Run

In April of 2023, I set out on the best road trip of my life, a mission my brother jokingly called "Wolf Ball Run" in homage to the famous Burt Reynolds film, Cannonball Run. The objective was to keep a promise I'd made to two of my wolves. Aqutaq, my mature female, loved puppies. As she was getting older, I wanted to give her the opportunity to enjoy another pup before it was too late.

In addition, my prime male, Iqniq, who was turning four, had confided in me that he was a big boy with all his parts and that he really needed a girlfriend, or, as he put it, two girlfriends. He said, "I'm a big boy, I'm a strong boy, I can handle two girlfriends." Today, Iqniq realizes he bit off a bit more than he could chew, but to accommodate the needs of my other wolves, I set off on an incredible journey.

As I mentioned in the introduction, the preferred method for working with very high-content wolf dogs or wolves is to get them while they're very young. Unlike domestic dogs, who are much more adaptable to changing circumstances early in their lives, wolves develop differently. Taking advantage of these minor developmental differences allows people like me to do much more with wolves as they age.

My plan was simple but challenging. Kit out a small travel trailer—appropriately labeled "Wolf Pup," courtesy of the manufacturer—with all the equipment necessary to manage two tiny wolf puppies, then get them. The animals I was acquiring came from two locations: one in the central states and the other further north.

As you might imagine, getting animals this small when they're particularly vulnerable can be challenging—even more so if you're on the road. The tiny trailer I rented looked like a small veterinary hospital equipped with everything I could think of in case something went wrong.

In addition to the most comprehensive medical kit anyone this side of an ambulance carried, I had IV bags with fluids, baby bottles, and nipples of every size since it's sometimes difficult to get new pups to latch on to a bottle, and a suite of medications, including prednisone, in case I ran into some medical emergency far from the security of our regular veterinarian's office.

Sunny Wolf

Siqiniq, or Sunny as I call her, was just seven days old when I first held her in my hands. She was tiny, fully furred, and her eyes were not yet open. In the wild, wolves are typically born in a den, selected and excavated by the breeding female. In general, only the breeding female and the pups use the den. Occasionally, juvenile females from prior years or female siblings of the breeding female will enter the den to help care for the pups or provision the breeding female with regurgitated or dragged-in meat.

During this initial development period, the tiny puppies are blind, and their hearing isn't fully developed. But their sense of smell is working perfectly. The smells and sounds of that dark, protected den are the first information a pup needs to survive. Unlike the protected lives of most domestic canines, a wolf's world is filled with deadly threats—especially during their earliest days of life.

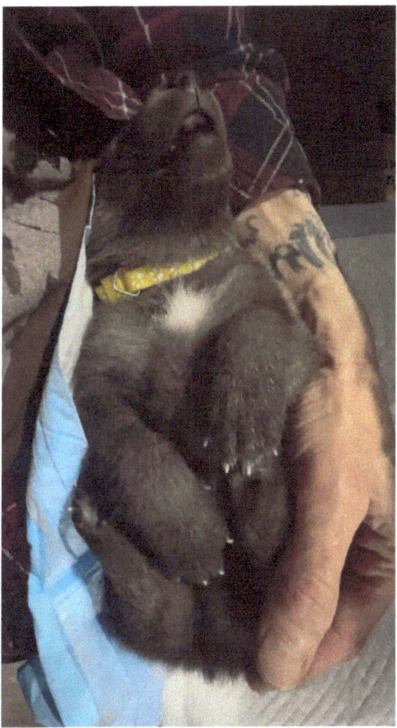

Siqiniq "Sunny" at ten days old. The extra time I got to spend bonding with Sunny during our "Wolf Ball Run" created an even stronger bond between the two of us.

A Baby Bottle and a Transformative Insight

On the second night in the trailer, after I'd given Sunny a bottle, I had a mind-blowing revelation. As I watched the tiny pup curled up in the bed of blankets on the table before me, I saw that she appeared to be dreaming. Her nose was twitching; the muscles in her face were twitching; her little paws opened and shut as if to run.

But then I thought, what could this puppy be dreaming about? She'd had no life experiences. All she knew were those first few days nursing with her mother, her time in my hands and on my chest, and nursing on the tiny baby bottles I'd prepared.

So, what could be going on in that little brain that would provoke these responses? And then I realized that this tiny wolf was writing the most critical early layers of her wolf operating system. Her brain was processing the sounds and smells and the sensations of me—of where we were—of what food she was given—all data that an early wolf brain needs to know what is safe and what is unfamiliar and, therefore, dangerous.

My wife and I had long known certain tricks to help accommodate our animals—including leveraging their incredible sense of smell to help anchor them to us—but this was the first time I'd seen this process in action: watching the absorption of information and neurological processes burning it into fundamental layers of this tiny being's consciousness.

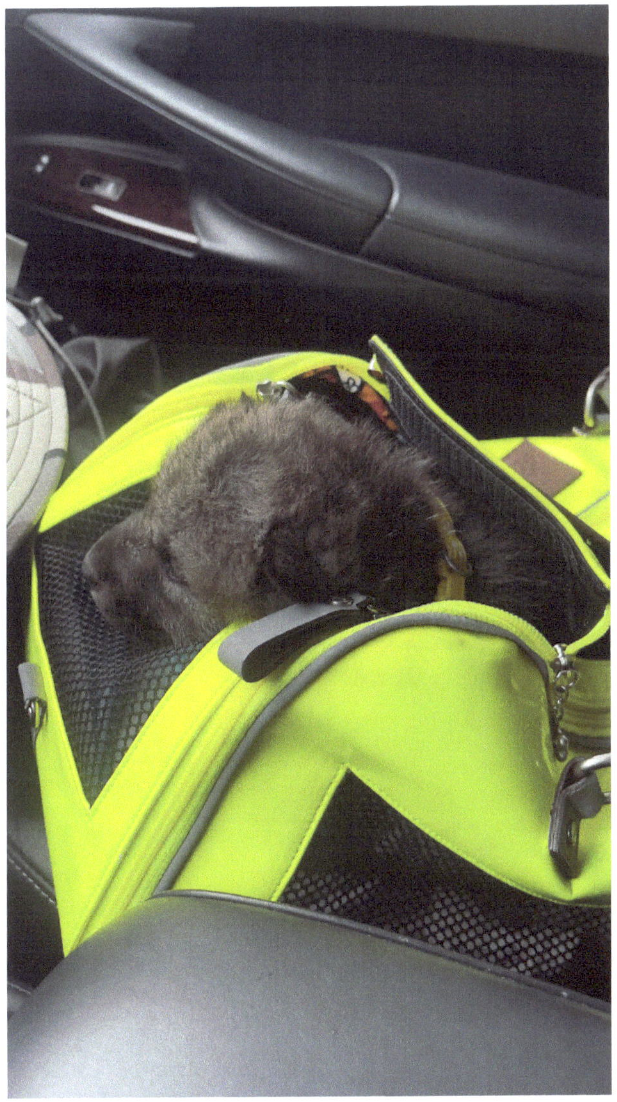

A tiny Siqinq peeking out from the carrier on the way to pick up her adopted sister, Taqqiq "Moonie."

Wolfy Wisdom from a Tiny Puppy

This revelation was so profound that tears started streaming down my face; I couldn't believe what I was seeing or understanding. This discovery opened my eyes to new ways to leverage my knowledge to improve my relationships with animals. Ultimately, it crystallized my thinking for the book you're holding now and led me to a greater understanding of the basis for canine behaviors. The insight I gleaned in this moment gave me a key to human understanding. Ultimately, what I discovered set the stage for me, and hopefully for you, to build deeper and better bonds within our mixed-species family groups so that we can coexist not just in harmony, but with joy.

On the bottle. Bottle feeding a tiny Siqiniq. Not only is bottle feeding essential for achieving the deepest possible bond with wolves or high-content wolfdogs, but it's also a critical part of providing them with the nutrition they need.

Taqqiq "Moonie" the Wolf Who Chose Me

Moonie and me, the day she won me over for good.

When I add animals to our program, the process is careful and, almost without exception, planned years in advance. As someone with a highly complex project that incorporates multiple generations of animals living together, my wife and I are highly selective. We typically arrange the opportunity to carefully evaluate the pups in a litter to make sure that the animals joining our family are appropriate for our objectives and compatible both genetically and temperament-wise with one another.

When it came to Siqiniq "Sunny," she was an obvious choice for many reasons. She was the largest and most robust pup in her litter, and even at just ten days old, she was already inclined to be more confident and affectionate than her litter mates. In other words, for my purposes, she was a genetic champion.

But not Moonie. When I arrived at the second location on my planned journey, my friend held up a big gray puppy and said, "Here's your girl." Like Sunny, this pup was the obvious genetic champion of her litter. Big. Bold. Larger even than the male puppies she'd been born with. She was, in common dog parlance, the pick of the litter.

But in the days I was helping my friend with the arduous task of nursing nine small pups, this tiny black puppy was laser-focused on me to the point where my friend even commented that in all the years she'd been raising animals, she'd never seen such a young pup so keen on a person. At times, after I'd given her a bottle, she'd crawl out of the warmth of the puppy pile and approach the edge of the pen closest to where I was sitting.

Even though she wasn't the obvious choice for my project, I began to feel an irrational attachment to her and her determination to hold my attention. It got to the point where I seriously began to question whether the pick of the litter, whom I'd nicknamed Big Bertha, was the animal that belonged with me.

Finally, seeing my indecision, my friend suggested I put "Bertha" in with Sunny to see if they were compatible. Amazingly, even at less than 20 days old, it was clear they weren't. Both girls began posturing and attempting to dominate each other. Then, I put "the little black girl" in with Sunny, and they curled up against one another and went to sleep.

Moments after introducing them, Moonie and Sunny curl up and doze off, sealing the deal that these two pups were Iqniq's future girlfriends.

It was decided, once again, as with Iqniq, that my pick of the litter ended up being the smallest and least robust puppy. Had it not been for her obvious efforts to win me over, I doubt if Moonie would have been the pup that joined my family.

Interestingly, just like Iqniq, starting off small doesn't mean you stay that way. In just the last few weeks, as they head into their second winter, Moonie has obviously eclipsed Sunny in size, and her personality is even bigger than she is, earning her the nickname MoonieBadger the Angry Weasel for her somewhat fierce and feisty disposition.

Moonie, showing her Angry Weasel tendencies, makes sure an eight-week-old Nunar-juaq understands his place in the family hierarchy.

Who's Who in Our Personal Zoo

In addition to Sunny and Moonie, whom I've described above, we currently have four other furred family members, and a fifth, Bixby, recently passed, who set the stage for our current success. Here are their stories.

Bixby - King Wooly

Prime Bixby at two years old.

When I talk about canine culture and use the term "mentor dog," my thoughts always turn to Bixby, our giant wooly malamute boy who taught me more about dogs than any other canine ever will. He was my best friend, wingman, the "Seven-Star Sheriff," and the unquestioned leader of our canine companions.

He was seven months older than Aqutaq, and she looked up to him, mirrored him, deferred to him, and loved him deeply. Bixby was one of those unique dogs possessed of such deep empathy that he never required a single day of dedicated training, yet behaved as though he'd exceeded any level of canine education available. If any dog could read my mind, Bixby was the one.

Somehow, he understood the rules of the house, and he rigorously enforced them on Aqutaq, Iqniq, and even Sunny and Moonie. The greatest tragedy for us is that canines don't live forever, but even in the end, Bixby made it easy for us.

Although he had slowed a bit with age, it wasn't until the last two weeks of his life that time got the best of him. He passed peacefully without intervention in his favorite place, Thanya's kitchen, with both of us beside him. His presence still looms large in our lives, as he rests on our property in a memorial I built, and through the culture he helped instill in Aqutaq and Iqniq before he left us.

Bixby on his sixth birthday. On his special day, Bixby always enjoyed a day off from "Wolf Sheriff" duty. We usually went someplace special, just he and I, so he could enjoy being a dog without the responsibilities of mentoring wolves.

The Story of Princess Bitchy Pants - Aqutaq

Her Royal Highness, Aqutaq, our Princess Bitchy Pants in all her regal glory.

In April of 2011, we added Aqutaq to our family group. For this round of wolves, she was preceded only by our giant Wooly Malamute boy, Bixby, who was just seven months older. She started off as a "bitchy pants" straight away. Within 20 minutes of having her in the car with me, she latched onto my septum, causing my nose to start gushing blood. And then, while she was still latched on to my nose, she proceeded to poop all over my lap. It was the beginning of a beautiful relationship.

Aqutaq, whose name means ice cream in the ancient Inuit Yupik dialect, is principally an Arctic wolf. And she has been one of the most interesting yet challenging I've had. To say she's spicy is an understatement. I regularly tell her it's okay to be spicy. "You can be jalapeño," I say. She looks right at me as if to say, "Sorry, dude, I'm ghost pepper." And she proves it by biting me almost every day. Now, to be fair, her bites are not intended to cause me serious damage, but rather, they're akin to when you're tickling or tormenting your domestic partner, and they slap your hand away. Only her slap leaves a mark almost every time.

Because I had the good fortune of raising her only with a single and powerful mentor malamute, Bixby, we were able to accomplish some extraordinary things with this girl. She's been on stage at a tech conference in front of over 10,000 people. She's done school programs, campfire talks, national park events, and for me, perhaps most exciting, because of my bond with her, I was even able to take her to remote locations and let her completely free to run and return, including a few sessions with a GoPro mounted on her chest. All of my animals are smart, but she has always been next-level, which means she's also been next-level destructive.

One of her most memorable destructions was when we were planning a Christmastime visit to Wild Spirit Wolf Sanctuary to help my friends out when they were short of staff. The night before, I had managed to break a key off in a rooftop carrier lock, and after spending hours in the dark trying to solve the problem, I gave up and went to bed. This lapse proved to be a big mistake. When I woke up at 7 a.m. the following day to try to attack the roof carrier problem in daylight, I was horrified to see what looked like a yard sale all over the habitat. I had forgotten to close the door. Aqutaq had taken it upon herself to unburden the vehicle of everything I'd loaded, but worst of all, she unburdened it of both driver and passenger seat belts, cleaving them clean off. We didn't leave for the trip that day or the next, as I spent hours chasing down replacement safety belts so that we could enjoy our excursion without undue risk.

Many of the terms I use in my books, including "wolf haircut" and "wild box," come directly from our life with her.

When Aqutaq was eight, we decided to add another Lupine family member and brought Iqniq into our group. It was amazing to see an animal that rejects every other dog with extreme prejudice instantly adopt this beautiful tiny black wolf puppy and take him for her own.

Her maternal instincts have persisted, and now she's had the opportunity to be the surrogate mother of not just Iknik but Sunny, Moonie, Nepenthe, and even Nuni. She's now 13 and a half, and with the exception of a little arthritis in her knee, she's as feisty and robust as ever, and I hope she continues to share my life and my sofa for many years to come.

For people wondering why we call her Princess BitchyPants, it's because she's particularly spicy when it comes to other dogs. Ever since she hit maturity at two years old, she's shown zero tolerance for any canine who isn't an immediate family member. She's fiercely protective of her territory and family, especially puppies, and she considers herself my equal partner and my wife her sister, but not her boss. Working with her and spending tens of thousands of hours in direct contact with her, particularly in the backcountry, has added immeasurably to my knowledge of wolf behavior and the subtleties of canine social family dynamics. If any creature on earth has been my muse, it's her.

Iqniq's Story, from Runt to "Monstah-Wolf"

"Monstah-Wolf" Iqniq in deep snow sporting a Margo-Tech tracking collar we helped test for the company.

When I got Iqniq—whose name means "Meteor" or "Fireball" in Inuktitut—he was tiny. It was a planned acquisition from a friend. I had already committed to acquiring a black-phase male puppy (usually, wolf pups are born gray and will grow up to be gray or tan, but if a puppy is born with black fur, they will stay black; we call these animals "black-phase") if one was born. The breeding was so carefully planned that we captured the actual mating of Iqniq's parents on video. (When canines mate, there's a brief period where they're actually stuck together. This is called a copulatory tie.) Sometimes, I tell Iqniq, "I knew you when you were tiny. I knew you when they made you."

I was on-site to help with the litter within days of Iqniq's birth, and we pulled the puppies at ten days old after witnessing the mother carrying a single stillborn pup. We began to worry the first-time mother might be struggling with the litter. Luckily, only one pup died, and the other five were in condition excellent.

Although I had the option of the pick of the litter, Iqniq was the only black male and the runt, but I didn't care. He was perfect. I knew that he would have the best possible life and chance to achieve his genetic potential with me. Five years later, he's the largest wolf I've ever owned and one of the largest wolves on record, topping the scales at nearly 160 pounds.[3]

After nursing the litter on site for about two and a half weeks, I was ready to bring Iqniq home. I also brought one of Iqniq's sisters to a friend's wolf preserve in Colorado. It was quite an adventure taking two little wolf puppies through multiple airports and changing them out at Koala Care stations in men's rooms. To say I got a few sideways glances is putting it mildly. But the real adventure began the moment I brought Iqniq in the door.

---

3   https://www.adfg.alaska.gov/index.cfm?adfg=wildlifenews.view_article&articles_id=503

With an iPhone for scale, a 24-day-old Iqniq sleeps on my lap.

Hi, mom! My wife, Thanya, the other half of our wolf care team, meets Iqniq for the first time upon picking the two of us up at the airport.

Nepenthe's Story

Puppy Nepenthe being the perfect malamute and enjoying a trip with Mom and Dad.

Nepenthe is the only domestic dog in our family group. She's a purebred Alaskan Malamute who shares her birthday, February 4th, with wolf mama Thanya Starr. Her name is especially appropriate for two reasons.

First, she is the future Immaculate Bride of our beloved Bixby, who passed away in April at nearly 14 years old. Bixby, also a purebred Alaskan Mala-mute, was such a spectacular animal that we decided to bank his sperm to preserve his extraordinary genetics. While we weren't planning on getting another Malamute so soon, when we saw Nepenthe and learned of her birthday, we felt it was fate that she should join our family.

Secondly, Bixby's name came from a famous bridge near Big Sur, where I used to live, and Nepenthe is a remarkable restaurant on the coast not far from where I used to live. Nepenthe has more than lived up to her name, helping Thanya and me in our time of deep despair at the loss of a once-in-a-lifetime-dog and beloved family member. She is the most cuddly, sweet, affectionate, and joyful Malamute I've had.

For the most part, Malamutes tend to be somewhat stubborn and slightly aloof canines, but Nepenthe has a very sweet, sociable personality that was just what we needed as we mourned the loss of our eldest furry child. While Bixby was a perfect gentleman, a Malamute who would literally guard my steak if I left it on an ottoman, Nepenthe is a little unruly. After all, she's had terrible, wolfy role models.

Nepenthe's story is so unique that I've written a children's book dedicated to her and her unruliness called *The Little Malamute Raised by Wolves*. It will be available simultaneously as this book gets published on all the same platforms. It features beautiful illustrations of Nepenthe and all her wolfy family.

Snow Feet! A nine-week-old Nepenthe gets her zoom on during a ski day with Dad.

Nunarjuaq, the Rescue Puppy

Nunarjuaq at five-months-old.

Nunarjuaq's name means "of the land or earth," but we call him Nuni, and he nearly cost me my marriage. After adding puppies Sunny and Nuni in 2023 and then Nepenthe in 2024, the last thing I planned was adding another wolfy creature to my family group. But sometimes, you just have to bite the bullet.

Nuni's background is somewhat tragic, and I don't have all the details of his early life. Unlike most of my family member additions, Nuni was not on our new family member schedule.

A friend of mine, who specializes in exotic felids, received a message from someone asking if she was interested in acquiring a Siberian tiger. She wasn't. But then they asked if she wanted a wolf. Curious, she asked for details. Somehow, this puppy had fallen into the hands of people involved in the illegal exotic animal trade. My friend reached out to me, concerned that this beautiful little guy would end up in a cage in some drug dealer's living room, and we began to plot his release.

The folks involved in the sale were relatively unsavory. They did not want to meet me in the United States, and the last thing I was going to do was travel across an international border to meet people with sketchy backgrounds who I did not know. Eventually, we determined that the best non-U.S. ground would be to meet in the Blackfoot Indian Reservation in Browning, Montana.

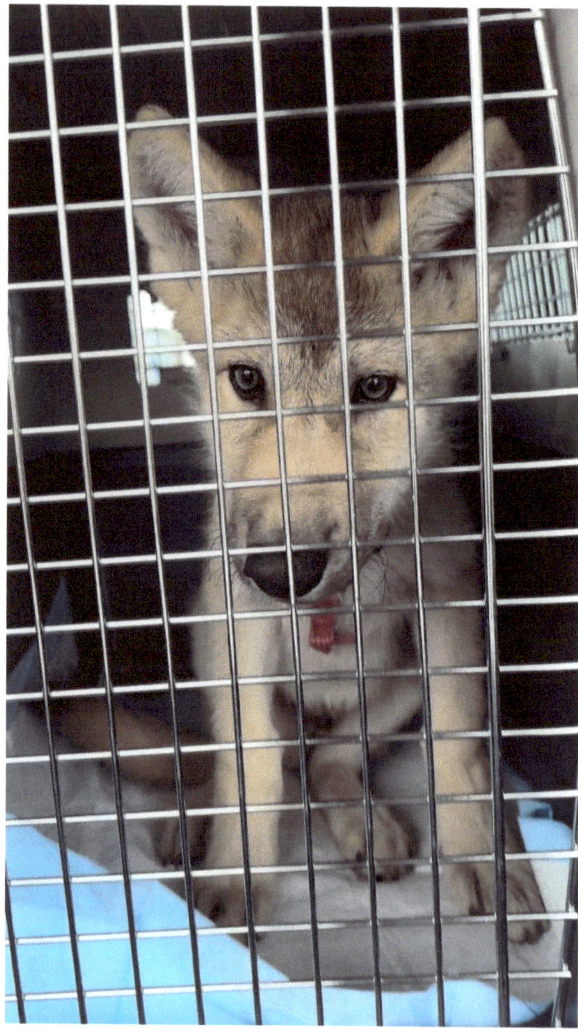

All Ears. Nunarjuaq, at the moment he joined his forever family.

After tense negotiations and my wife threatening to leave me more than once because she was afraid I wasn't going to come back alive, let alone with a new puppy, I met them in the IGA Grocery parking lot in the Blackfoot Tribal Reservation's sovereign territory. They pushed a crate across to me. Inside, I expected to find a terrified, traumatized animal that would require years of rehabilitation before he felt comfortable with me or anyone else. Instead, out popped one of the most sociable, fearless animals I've ever seen. Nuni is so brave that we nicknamed him Nuni No-Fucks because nothing seems to faze him. We like to joke that when they were handing out fucks to give, he didn't even bother to get in line. He'll walk right up to a car and let somebody pet him right out the window—something I've never had a wolf do in all the years I've been handling them.

I wish I had insights into his earliest days to understand how he was socialized to become such a self-assured and interesting animal. But just because he's confident doesn't mean he's not a challenge. He's the most intense, voracious eater of any animal I've had in 40 years.

Even now, after hand-feeding him for five months, I still have to wear gloves or take serious damage as he grabs food out of my hands. He's also going to be absolutely massive. He's not even eight months old yet and already weighs over a hundred pounds, with another year and a half of development still to go. He could easily top the scales at 160 and potentially even more.

Because I got him at seven weeks old instead of seven days, I have concerns about the strength of my bond with him during difficult situations like the breeding season. Except for Jake, whom I didn't raise from a pup, all my other animals have always been fine with me during wolf breeding season. But I do have my concerns about Nuni. Between his size and his confident disposition, in my world, it's the big, confident animals you sometimes have to worry about. But we'll take it as it comes, and no matter how his personality turns out once he's fully mature, we'll adapt to him because that's the name of the game. When you commit to an animal, you commit to that animal for its entire life.

Precious Cargo - the team at Alaskan Airlines did a remarkable job ensuring Nunarjuaq had an uneventful journey.

Safe at last! Nunarjuaq rests on our sofa moments after receiving our veterinarian's "all clear" to introduce him to his new life and family.

Aqutaq and Iqniq carefully monitor a tiny Sunny as she takes her earliest steps in our large habitat.

Chapter 3

Why You Should Raise Puppies Like Wolves Do

Wolves Are the Best Parents

Wolves are some of the best parents in the animal kingdom. When people say, "It takes a village," in reference to humans, I say, "It takes a pack," when it comes to wolves. In any given wolf family group, every member plays a role in protecting, feeding, and upbringing that year's offspring. In what is known as a "simple pack," which is how every wolf pack initially forms, a male and female wolf meet in unoccupied territory, decide they like each other, and set out to create and raise a family.

Unlike dogs, which can have multiple estrus cycles a year, wolves only come into heat once, always in late winter or early spring. If puppies were born at any other time, their chances of survival would be very slim. Wolf pups must be born in the spring when the weather is temperate, and food sources are plentiful for the adults. By "easy food sources," I mean the other animal babies born at the same time as the wolf pups and the animals weakened by the previous winter and still vulnerable to predation.

Like dogs, wolves have a 63-day gestation period. The pups are typically born in a den chosen and prepared by the breeding female. These dens can vary greatly, from a simple depression under a fallen tree to complex, multi-generational dens maintained and expanded over many years. However, these dens are typically located near fresh water, central to good hunting areas, and offer a view that allows the wolves to spot both prey and fellow predators as they approach.

Wolf Moms Run the Show

Wolf family groups are generally matriarchal. Contrary to the old alpha myth, the breeding male does not run the show. Alpha males might be seen as the leaders, but the breeding female wolf truly holds the family together. I see the female as the brains of the operation, with the males being the muscle. Except in unusual circumstances, the female is the only adult wolf that spends much time inside the den. A den she selects and prepares meticulously as the time for the birth of her puppies draws near.

I have been in multiple wolf dens, both dug and used by captive wolves and their wild counterparts. And I am always struck by how carefully excavated and thoughtfully located these birthing chambers tend to be. Typically, they are close to water, placed where the wolves can see the terrain, maintain concealment, and, if necessary, defend it. As the breeding female prepares to give birth, she'll often pull the hair from around her nipples so her pups can easily nurse right after birth. Wolves are wonderful mothers who take remarkable and selfless care of their pups, even under incredibly challenging circumstances.

Wolf puppies are born blind and partially deaf, but have all their fur and the sharpest little claws you can imagine. Their teeth are not yet exposed at birth. After giving birth, the mother carefully removes the placenta, nips off the umbilical cord right at each puppy's belly, and pushes them toward her nipples to nurse. She helps them urinate and defecate by licking their inguinal region and consumes the waste to keep the den clean. I've been inside active wolf dens, and it's always remarkable how clean the mother keeps them, even with a large litter of eight or more puppies.

For the most part, the post-parturition female doesn't leave the den except to relieve herself, drink water, or eat the food brought to her by her mate and other family members. However, if a female wolf gives birth alone because her mate has been killed after breeding, it presents an incredibly dire situation for the wolf family. The pups are highly vulnerable, and it is extremely difficult for the female to hunt enough to nourish herself and her puppies. Some of the saddest wolf stories involve a female who lost her mate and, as a result, lost her pups and even died of starvation herself.

In another data point that showcases just how vital the breeding female is to wolf family groups, a large-scale analysis I did of wolf pack longevity cross-referenced against wolf mortality from human causes determined that when people killed the breeding female, the rest of the pack disintegrated 74% of the time with additional follow on mortality. A similar study conducted by Kira Cassidy of the Yellowstone Wolf Project yielded similar data showing that reproduction in wolf family groups destabilized by human-related mortality was dramatically reduced.[4]

---

4   https://esajournals.onlinelibrary.wiley.com/doi/10.1002/fee.2597

Careful introduction: Aqutaq's first moments with puppy Iqniq. She went on to not only "adopt" him, but defend him against everyone, including my wife, Thanya, for the first few weeks of his life with us. For some reason, though, she was always at ease with me handling him.

Adopted mom. The joy and caring Aqutaq exhibited when I brought Iqniq home was something to behold. Understanding the social nature of wolves is one of the keys to cultivating the most fulfilling relationship between your dog and your family.

The struggle is real. Fatigue is evident on my face as I work tirelessly to duplicate the care wild wolves deliver to their puppies.

Applying This to Domestic Puppies

So, how does this apply to our more conventional puppies? When people like me acquire new wolf pups, I follow a very prescribed practice to ensure that the pup has the best possible life and the most comfortable family dynamic when forced to live in captivity with people for their entire lives. Generally, professionals like me prefer to get the pups very early—ideally when they're still nursing and before their eyes have even opened.

To accomplish this early socialization, these very young puppies are typically taken from their mother, and caretakers bottle-feed them every four hours for six to eight weeks. With large litters, this can be especially arduous. You'll quickly learn how good wolf mothers are when you try to replicate their efforts with a team of people, yet still struggle.

Our main concern initially is ensuring that the pups gain weight and become accustomed to the people who will care for them for the rest of their lives. The routine primarily involves feeding them, burping them, helping them go to the bathroom, cleaning them up, and holding them until it's time to start the process all over again.

It takes about 30 minutes to bottle-feed and clean each puppy. If you have a litter of eight puppies, this process takes about four hours. By the time you're done, the first puppy needs to be fed again, meaning you're pretty much going 24/7 with only short breaks in between. Fortunately, unless you're dealing with an unusual situation or the premature birth of a puppy, you won't have to endure this level of care with domestic dogs. However, there are certain practices I follow that I recommend for anyone with puppies.

There's No Substitute for Your Time

The first recommendation is to spend every possible waking moment with your very young puppy. Even if your pup is too small, too big, or too squirmy for you to hold for extended periods, you should try to stay as close to them as possible. Ideally, sleep with them or near them. Both my wife, Thanya, and I typically sleep in the crate with the puppies, just like a wolf mom would with her young. But if this is uncomfortable or impractical, I suggest placing the crate you're using to train your puppy as close as possible to where you sleep.

I model everything we do after how wolf family groups care for their puppies to form the most profound possible bond between the puppy and its human family. The more time you spend near your puppies now, the stronger that relationship will be for the rest of the animal's life. Even if you get your puppy at a more typical 8 or 10 weeks, there's still plenty of time to use this technique to benefit your family, so long as your pup isn't showing a strong, adverse reaction to being crated. It's not a big deal for a puppy to express a little anxiety and frustration if they're secured in a crate, but if you use the "crate-as-a-den" concept, where the crate is left open in a somewhat larger secure area, you're a lot less likely to have issues. We'll talk more about how to use crates in Chapter 5.

Integrate Your Whole Family

If you have kids, it's vitally important that they also spend as much time with the puppies as possible. It's equally important that your children treat the puppies gently and with respect. In multi-generation wolf family groups, the pups from prior years often remain with their families and become primary caretakers and babysitters. Yearling pups, who are not yet great hunters, usually play a critical role in caring for their younger siblings.

Especially if your children prevailed upon you to add a canine family member, it's **vital** to incorporate them into the care and training of your pups. Ideally, every member of your family will spend time with your dog, supply food and treats, and, most importantly, close companionship. In many ways, having all your family members participate in pup-rearing and the ongoing care of your dogs at any age simulates the wolf family dynamics that yield the close bonds wolves share with all their pack mates.

How Mature Animals Help You Raise Your Puppy

Our family has noticed an interesting self-selection process as we've added new pups over the years. Our matriarch, Aqutaq—who we affectionately call Princess BitchyPants—is a very spicy girl. She's now 13, but she hasn't slowed down a bit and is quick to let any dog that comes near her know that she means business. She's not very nice to canines that aren't part of our family, but she's an entirely different animal when it comes to puppies. She loves puppies, even those that aren't wolves, and she's always gentle and careful when they're around. The most amazing thing happened when we got her first puppy. That puppy, now five years old, is a male in his prime named Iqniq, which means "meteor" or "fireball" in Inuktitut.

Soft eyes: Aqutaq has always been our "spiciest" animal, but she had nothing but gentle eyes for puppy Iqniq.

Princess BitchyPants Adopts a Puppy

From the very second I drove into the driveway, Aqutaq's stern demeanor completely changed. Her face became soft and gentle, her motions slow and careful. Before I could get him in the door, she gently sniffed the tiny black bundle in my arms. It was immediately apparent that she would be his primary caretaker and always be careful with this little pup. During the many years I've had wolves, I've seen this self-selection process again and again, as these highly intelligent animals seem to naturally know their roles as they relate to their close-knit family groups.

Once I brought Iqniq into our home, I placed him in a secure dog bed and gave Aqutaq access. She immediately took possession of this tiny puppy as her own. For the first several weeks, I was the only person she would easily allow to approach him. She was even fiercely protective of him when my wife came, although she would relent and let her handle the pup while grumbling and acting nervous. Although she wasn't producing milk, when I started to wean him, she was essential in the transition from bottles to solid food.

How Wolf Pups Beg for Dinner

When wolves lick their parents' faces, they're begging for dinner, attempting to solicit regurgitation of partially digested meat, which is what the puppies initially eat once they stop consuming solely their mother's milk. I was amazed and fortunate to capture the first time puppy Iqniq solicited Aqutaq for a meal. I wouldn't have believed she would be willing or capable of regurgitating for him, but that's precisely what she did.

From then on, she was essential in the weaning process, providing the majority of Iqniq's calories by eating twice as much as she ordinarily would and then supplying half of it back to him in predigested, wolf-perfect form.

Puppies Beg the Same Way

So, what can we take from this behavior and apply it to our own dogs? One of the things that bonds wolf families is their collaborative hunting and sharing of food. Wolves don't fight each other for the choicest morsels on a kill—everyone gets to eat, and all the mature animals help provide food for the puppies.

Puppies will solicit any animal for a meal, and frequently, those animals oblige. The human analog to this with domestic dogs is that all family members should collaborate in feeding the new puppies. With very young pups, I do a lot of ad hoc feeding rather than designated mealtimes because that is more natural than the by-the-clock approach humans tend to employ. However, that can be inconvenient for people because it also means that crate training and housebreaking can become complicated since pups frequently need to use the restroom right after eating.

Everyone Should Feed Your Puppies

For people who wish to use established mealtimes, I suggest having more than one family member present the food to the puppies simultaneously. I'm a huge believer in hand feeding. Putting a bowl down in front of a puppy and letting them charge through the food has numerous drawbacks. The first is that puppies can eat too quickly and make themselves sick by swallowing air; in some cases, they can even become bloated due to this practice.[5] Secondly, by placing a bowl in front of the pup and giving the pup possession of the bowl, you're creating a dynamic where once the puppy has food, they own it.

In the wolf world, keeping possession of anything is a matter of life and death. So resource guarding, that is, aggressive behavior in puppies when they wish to retain control of something, whether it's food, a toy, or a bone, is not unusual but normal. However, it's undesirable for many reasons, not the least of which is that it is the most frequent reason people get bitten by their own dogs.[6]

---

5   While bloat is usually no big deal in puppies, analogous to burping human babies, this practice of gulping down food too quickly can be a dangerous habit if carried to adulthood where bloat can be fatal. This is especially true if you're feeding commercial food, especially kibble. While wolves can consume pounds of meat in seconds, their bodies are primed to digest protein whereas kibble is frequently implicated in serious and even fatal instances of a bloated stomach worsening to a condition called "torsion" that is invariably fatal if not immediately treated by a skilled emergency vet.

6   https://pmc.ncbi.nlm.nih.gov/articles/PMC2610618/#:~:text=Records%20of%20bites%20to%20111,dogs%20to%20obedience%20training%20classes

Hand-Feeding Reduces Resource Guarding

By hand-feeding your puppies and retaining control of their food, parceling it out a little at a time, you're sending a strong message that you control the resource and that all good things come from your hands. If hands are associated with the most positive things in a puppy's life, they're much less likely to bite them. My practice is to hand-feed our animals for not just weeks or months but years. I hand-fed Aqutaq, our current matriarch, more than 90% of her lifetime calories for the first seven years of her life. And I only stopped hand-feeding her every meal when Iqniq came, and I needed to devote much of that attention to him. Even now, I do a lot of hand-feeding with our animals to reaffirm that good things come from us. I also have a practice that when I reach into a bowl that the animal has, I bring something better. Animals are not nearly as likely to become defensive or aggressive toward your hands if there's always a better treat involved when those hands come toward them.

I do not feed kibble and do not recommend feeding kibble to puppies. I'll do a whole chapter about feeding later in this book, but for now, let me simply say that most commercial dog food is refuse generated by the human food industry, and it isn't even close to good nutrition or healthful, despite what the packages attempt to portray. At the end of this book, there will be recipes for all stages of your animal's life, but all canine diets should consist primarily of clean protein, moderate fat, and limited dark green leafy vegetables. There are modifications for puppies, but that's our base diet.

To wrap up the first part of caring for puppies like wolves, I'll break it down into simple steps.

1. Spend as much time as possible in close proximity to your puppy, including at night. It's essential to include all family members who will be living with your dogs. If your kids sleep in a different room and you want them to have as close and secure a bond as possible with their puppies,

it's not a bad idea to alternate the placement of the puppy from night to night so they become comfortable in close proximity to everyone.

2. Do not exclude your puppy from the social gatherings in your household. Even if you must contain your animals because they're bothersome to guests, it's better to keep them close to you than to segregate them outdoors, making them feel alienated from the family group.

3. Do not engage in any aversive conditioning. Our animals don't know what a correction looks like. For me, the most significant punishment that I ever deliver is something called shunning, and that's when Thanya and I turn our backs on the puppies and say, "Nope, we're over you right now. You're being naughty, and we don't like it," and we show them our backside. If they're being particularly onerous, we may segregate them to the secure kennel that encloses our entire back deck and close the door, so they're left alone briefly. Typically, simply being isolated from the rest of the family group is enough to get them to calm down and shape up almost immediately. Wolves and dogs are family animals. Wolves are not wolves without the pack; dogs consider humans their family. Exploit this for your benefit, and you'll have the best possible relationship with your dog.

4. Hand-feed everything for as long as you can. Control your dog's food and provide little bits at a time. One trick I use is always to carry some kind of treat in my pockets. So when puppies approach me and solicit me for food, I can dispense small treats regularly. Again, this encourages the closest bond possible, and a benefit is that it tunes your puppies into your behavior, no matter where you are or what you're doing. This practice can be life-saving if your puppy gets loose and you've lost control of your animal. If you've always got something yummy, your pup will probably stay close by or even come up to you because they want a treat.

5. Finally, be patient with puppies. They're rude and unruly. They don't know any better. Iqniq's original Instagram account was called "Rude Little Puppy," and Nuni is so much worse that I lovingly call him my personal demon. In addition to our matriarch, Aqutaq, I typically use mature Alaskan Malamutes as example-setting mentor dogs. During Iqniq's puppyhood, our Malamute was a giant male named Bixby, who I called "the Sheriff." He was the boss in the house, and Iqniq annoyed him to no end. Although he wasn't nearly as gentle or patient as Aqutaq, he did know how to keep puppies that were being rude in line.

Disciplining Unruly Puppies

It's somewhat tricky for humans to employ wolf discipline, but our approach to maintaining some semblance of decorum with puppies is similar to what their grown family members and siblings generally do. I growl. To others, it probably looks like I've got a few loose screws when a puppy's getting uppity and my wife or I bend toward them, bare our teeth, and act like a bigger wolf.

Typically, the response is immediate submission, and often, the puppies will roll over on their backs. When they're very small, they may even pee a little bit. Submission is the desired response. The big kids let the little kids know who the boss is in a firm but gentle way, never with anger—only at times with a tiny bit of annoyance. Humans can emulate this behavior without being rough on their puppies.

It is critical to remember that these are loving actions, not aggression. Puppies need guidance, and this is the language they understand.

The Best Reunions

One final note: when leaving your puppy behind, expect and work towards an exuberant greeting. When wolf families reunite after even brief times apart, their joy is evident and contagious. Even as I'm dictating this book, I'm coming home from a hike right now, and at this moment, I'm witnessing a greeting between the puppies I've walked and the big kids who stayed home. It's amazingly charming to see wolf pups greet their elders, and your puppies will try to greet you the same way if you let them. Let them. Nothing reaffirms social bonds like warm greetings after every absence. Plus, you get the best kisses, which is highly recommended.

Siqiniq "Sunny" and Taqqiq "Moonie" at five weeks old and looking wolfier every day.

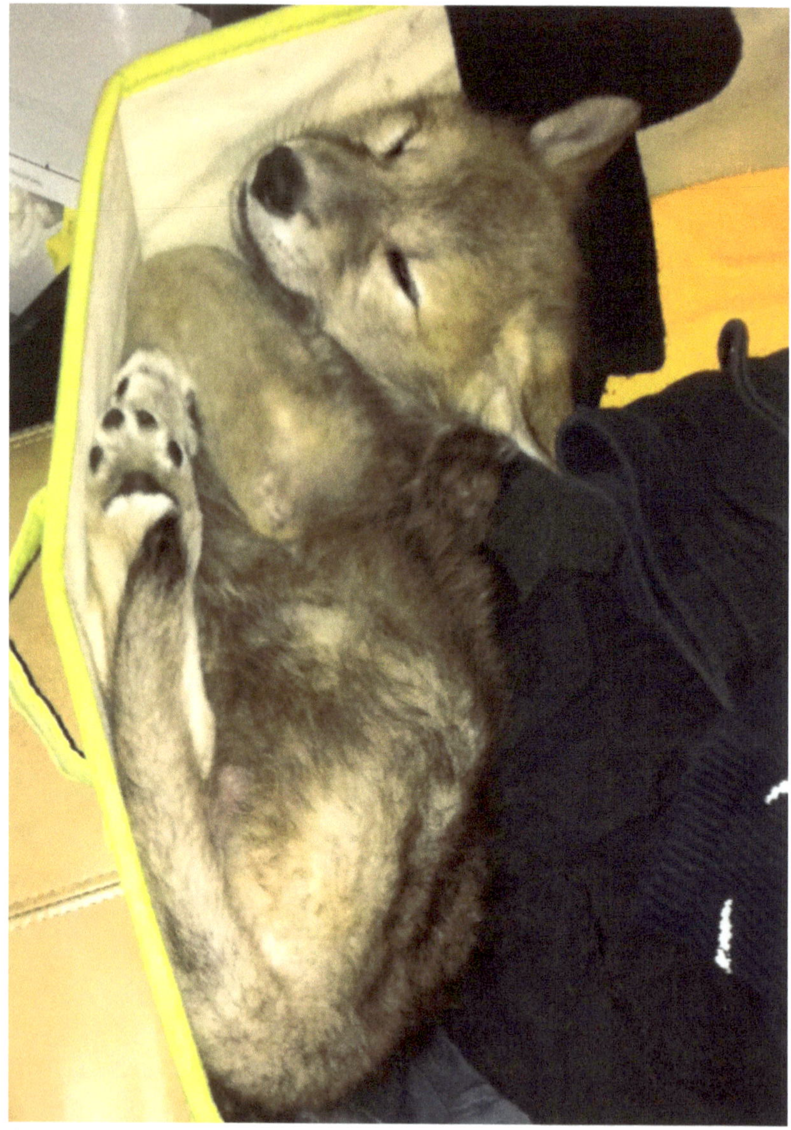

A tiny Aqutaq sleeping in our dirty laundry basket. What better way for your pup to learn how your family smells?

Chapter 4:

The Secret of Stinky Socks and Dirty Underwear

Wolf Pups Smell Their Way Into Their World

As I mentioned before, the first and most fully developed sense in newborn wolf pups and domestic dogs is olfaction or smell. The moment they breathe their first breaths, their sense of smell is acute. If you think about it, this makes sense. The most important thing for a newborn pup is to figure out where food is, who their family members are, and what their home smells like.

My experience watching one of my yearling wolves, Siqiniq "Sunny," dream when she was just a few days old and I was traveling with her to pick up her sibling, Taqqiq "Moonie," and realizing that her brain was processing and writing into her most important memory files the smell of me and what I was feeding her enlightened me to just how important this early process is. Those insights allowed me to do even better work with future puppies. Even before I picked up Sunny, my wife and I knew that the smell of our intimate clothing was particularly important to our wolves and dogs. I consistently leverage that knowledge to benefit our animals.

Letting Your Pups Smell the Real You

As our knowledge increased and our practices became more refined, I took this knowledge to the extreme. I asked myself, what do I really smell like? Unlike animals, whose scents are typically genuine, humans doctor their odors through chemical and textile means. We cover ourselves in clothing, prevent ourselves from perspiring, and slather odorous compounds, from lotion to face cream to perfume and more, on our bodies from head to toe. Most of the time, we don't smell like ourselves; we smell like the products we purchase. However, this isn't the case for the socks and underwear you've worn that day. As anyone with a keen sense of smell is acutely aware, your old socks and your worn underpants generally don't pass the sniff test when you pull them off in the evening.

Dirty Laundry - Your Best Puppy-Raising Tool

While I'm not particularly keen on sleeping with soiled garments, I can't say the same for my animals. Whenever I travel to pick up a puppy, I want to ensure that they have the benefit of their contact with me and the smells of my body, and that of my wife and our home. I often joke that I always get the puppy breath milkshake—that is the unique smell of puppy breath, which some people detest, but which both my wife and I adore—and she gets what's left at the bottom of the cup. But I do my best to level the playing field by bringing her laundry along for the ride.

Instead of spending money on dog blankets and dog beds for my newborn puppies, I pack their crate and puppy carrier with the stinkiest unwashed laundry I can find. The minute I acquire a young animal, I line their travel containment with the smelliest clothes I can find. The objective is to give them that crucial information in the most potent way possible the minute they're in my care. In much the same way that the smell of the mother wolf and the den anchors new puppies to their family group, the scent of our dirty laundry and stinky socks does the same for our new puppies.

I continue this practice for the first several months of the animal's life; the typical duration pups routinely use a den. Even when they're older, I rely on the smell of our worn clothing to help ease stress in unfamiliar situations. By consistently providing a garment that smells strongly of us, even when we're not present, our animals receive the olfactory cue that helps them understand that we're still there and gives the implication that we're coming back. Of all the tricks in this book I'll share with you, this is one of my favorites, because it's funny and easy to apply. You're going to have to wash your clothes anyway, so why not put them to good use in the interim? Instead of our clothes going from our bodies to the hamper and then to the washer, they go from our bodies to the wolf crate and then to the washer. It's a short detour that pays giant dividends.

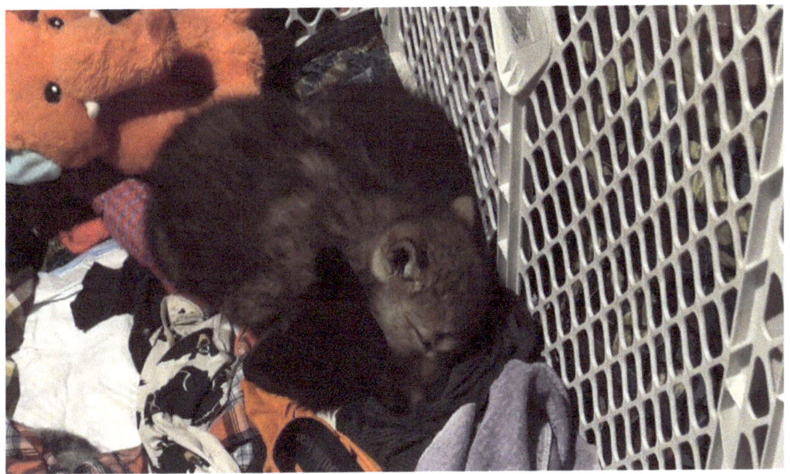

Ensconced in our smell, Sunny and Moonie benefit from our odorous underwear.

Your Hoodie - Your Pup's Favorite Security Blanket

As our animals get older, I do the same thing. Anytime they're going to be exposed to something unfamiliar, and especially if I'm not going to be with them, I leave our garments to help them adapt. Typically, our animals never stay at a vet unattended, and of course, there's no such thing as dog daycare or overnight accommodations for wolves. But if I had to check an animal in for emergency veterinarian overnight care, I would do so with dirty laundry to help anchor the animal and reduce any fear associated with our absence in an unfamiliar location.

So, what's the wolf wisdom for your new pups and your more mature animals? Simple.

- Give them your dirty clothes.
- Suffuse them in your scent.
- Let them become intimately familiar with the way your body actually smells.

Because I'm so deep in what I do, I take this even a little further, and I typically don't use any product that alters the smell of my body. I also shower a little less frequently than most people, so my animals know how I genuinely smell. I understand that these decisions pay massive dividends for my canines' emotional well-being and the bond we maintain throughout their lives.

Snuggled up in our dirty laundry, Moonie and Sunny sleep peacefully with Aqutaq standing guard.

They haven't even been in the crate for five minutes, yet both Sunny and Moonie look like hardened inmates!

Chapter 5

Dens, not Jails

Especially if you've acquired a youthful canine, crates can be one of your most valuable allies, but only if you use them correctly. I can't tell you how often I've seen crate failures associated with people who don't understand the purpose of a crate or how to use it for the benefit of your pup. Of course, a crate is a safe place to contain your animal and prevent it from doing undesirable things in your home or vehicle. But that's a side benefit and should not be the primary purpose of a crate.

As discussed in previous chapters, wolf pups are invariably born in some type of den-like situation, whether in a burrow, a cave, a root ball under a tree, a shed, or some other confined and cozy place. Their earliest life is spent almost entirely nestled in a dark and confined area. It's the safest place in the world for a newborn puppy, well-defended by its family, and kept clean and secure by the mother wolf. There is no door in a den, and when pups attempt to leave against the wishes of their mother or family members, they're gently picked up by the scruff of their neck and carefully carried back to safety.

We can leverage this behavior to yield significant benefits, but we can also make a crate a place of frustration, anxiety, and fear. How things go is up to you, but if you follow my advice, your chances of making a crate your pup's favorite safe space will increase immeasurably.

Puppies, in general, are a challenge. Wolf puppies are a hundred times worse. They are agile, destructive, and intelligent. It's imperative to keep them contained. Here's the crating practice I employ that has yielded significant success with our animals.

As we discussed before, the bedding for the crate should be your stinky stuff. What smells like us smells like home and is a source of comfort and contentment. Don't put freshly washed towels or pee pads in your crate. You'll be giving up a significant olfactory advantage. And unless your puppies are very young and quite small, don't place them in a crate and lock them down. This sense of confinement and separation from their caretakers can provoke an anxious reaction, causing the crate to become anathema in short order.

Instead, place the crate in a larger, contained environment. When our puppies are tiny, I like the plastic puppy pens I call Puptagons. When they get a little bigger, I employ wire-framed X-pens that can be shaped free-form. The crate should be a source of security and good feelings, and it's easy to accomplish this. By placing an open crate in a slightly larger containment, the puppy can hide in the crate or play in a slightly roomier environment.

The added benefit of this is that you can put puppy pads in one portion of your playpen, and if you're lucky, your small pups will gravitate towards the pads to relieve themselves, keeping the crate relatively clean. Typically, I try to concentrate the area with the pads away from where I enter the x-pen or where the pups exit so that I avoid the joy of cleaning a "poo-foot" when a pup accidentally steps in poop and then tracks the mess everywhere.

Toys and desirable treats should always be placed inside the crate, with the idea that puppies are continuously rewarded for willfully going into and spending time in the crate. **Never pull your animal out of their crate; nothing a pup takes into their crate should be removed unless the puppy readily relinquishes it, except, of course, anything that could cause serious harm.** But even in those dire situations, it is better to trade than take what you're trying to recover so that you don't inadvertently create a resource-guarding fixation on something your pup shouldn't have.

Crates should never be used as punishment. Doing so completely defeats their purpose and will almost certainly yield a result opposite your intention.

If you do things right, when you give your puppy a bone, it will retreat to its crate to enjoy it in private. When the pup feels uneasy, it will retreat to the crate to feel secure. By ensuring that a crate is always associated with positive experiences, on those rare occasions when your animal needs to be confined to a crate, they are much more likely to accept their confinement willingly rather than attempt to claw their way to freedom.

As your animals mature and no longer need to be confined within your home, leaving the crate as an acceptable hideaway is still a solid practice. You'd be surprised how many animals will choose to hang out in their crates for extended periods throughout their lives because they know it's their particular spot.

My brother, who specializes in rescuing cattle dogs, noted that with his recent rescue, Smidge, at five months of age, was already too old to easily use a crate. He opted NOT to put the work into conditioning her to use a crate for sleeping, etc., since she was already good about not urinating or defecating in their home.

However, he notes that they always fed her in a crate, and even now, she will happily trot to the crate, which is in their den, to enjoy projects or meals. "It's particularly funny when she takes an Amazon box filled with paper and treats to work on it "in peace" in her crate," he told me.

In short, crates should be seen as dens, not jails. Crate experiences should always be rewarding, and crates should always be used positively, not negatively. In fact, for us, locking an animal out of a crate is more akin to an aversive condition than locking one in. Even some of my mature wolves have continued to enjoy spending time in crates, especially when they have something particularly tasty.

Here's how to make sure your pups love their crates:

- Put the best rewards, new toys, favorite treats, etc., inside your pup's crate

- Line the crate with your dirty clothes instead of freshly washed towels or puppy pads.

- Maintain open access to the crate at all times. If you need to confine a tiny pup, put the open crate in a confined area, like a puppy pen.

- Do not use the crate as a form of punishment, EVER.

- Do not force your animal into a crate against their will. If you need to crate a pup in an emergency, bait them in, don't force them in.

- Do not drag a pup out of their crate. It's THEIR safe space.

- Do not remove something a puppy has taken into a crate while the pup has it, unless the pup willingly relinquishes it or gives it up in trade. You may need to act quickly if the pup has something that can harm it. Still, it's far better to trade or bait the puppy out of the crate than to violate the security of the crate, as this can create new challenges, including defensive aggression, or stimulate resource-guarding behaviors.

To accustom your pup to being confined in a crate, you need to do this gradually for short periods while you are present and with rewards that keep the pup occupied. I like Kongs, beefy bones, filled Toppl's (a product made by a Montana Company called WestPaw[7]), or bully sticks (which I call Peeper Bones because it's funnier, and it's true!).

---

7   https://www.westpaw.com/products/toppl-treat-toy

Safe Space - Even though he's now over seven months old, Nunarjuaq still retreats to the security of his crate to enjoy a snack.

Early exposure: to help our animals get used to as many things as possible before they become naturally fearful, I take them everywhere. Above, I've got Iqniq in an "ergo-baby" carrier, and I'm taking him into a pet-friendly hardware store when he's not yet two weeks old.

Chapter 6:

Novelty and Neophobia

Neophobia and Why It Matters to Wild Wolves

Neophobia is the fear of new things. In the world of wolves, new things often mean danger, trouble, and death. That shiny new object with a strange smell could easily be a trap with lethal consequences. An unfamiliar noise on a strange strip of asphalt might be an oncoming vehicle that could end a wolf's life in a heartbeat. Once pups are out of the den and begin exploring their big new world, the risk of encountering something unfamiliar and lethal increases exponentially.

When pups initially emerge from the den, they are closely monitored by their parents and siblings and are generally well protected. They are not permitted to venture far. If they do, a more mature wolf will frequently grab them by the scruff of the neck and carefully carry them back to the area where they are most protected. But as the pups grow bigger and more difficult to contain, this job becomes harder and eventually impossible. Nature has a solution for this problem: during the first eight to twelve weeks of a wolf pup's life, they are not really afraid of much. They don't have a significant reason to be.

However, the window for accepting the new and unfamiliar starts to close at about twelve weeks, and by sixteen weeks, it's pretty well slammed shut.[8] The reason for this behavior in wolves is that this timing coincides with their ability to move further from the den, and the challenges wolf parents might have in keeping multiple exploring pups safe when they start to spread out.

For people like me who work with wolves, we attempt to compress everything we can think of that our pups need to accept into those fourteen weeks when they're most receptive to unfamiliar things, such as exposure to loud music, automobiles, other dogs, unfamiliar people, garbage trucks, trash cans, and vacuum cleaners. Our list is long and exhaustive. The better we do at exposing our pups to all of these unfamiliar things early, the more likely we won't have problems later.

But you can't think of everything...

An "Oh, Shit!" Moment

It was late August 2013 when I learned this, with some embarrassing results. Aqutaq, our Arctic wolf puppy, was a little over five months old, and we were taking a road trip to visit family and attend an athlete's reunion from my professional sporting career. After a long day in the car, we pulled up to the Westin Hotel at Beaver Creek. We were specifically staying at that hotel because of its exceptional dog-friendly policies. We figured a wolf pup wouldn't be a big deal.

Unfortunately, as we exited our vehicle in the reception driveway of this fancy hotel, other guests noticed that we were unloading what looked like a wolf. They began to gather around, ask questions, and take pictures. Had Aqutaq still been in the vehicle, this probably wouldn't have been a big deal. Unfortunately, she was already leashed up and on the ground. The unfamiliar location, coupled with the excessive attention, sent her into a state of pure terror, her natural "neophobic" inclinations taking over. It was too much stimulation, all unfamiliar, and all at the same time.

The people, the unfamiliar environment, cameras flashing, cars passing by, and valets peppering us with questions were too much for our girl. She did what any terrified wild animal would do: she fear-pooped. The phrase "oh,

8   https://www.sciencedirect.com/science/article/pii/S0003347215002250

shit" comes from the fact that even the best of us, when faced with a sufficiently terrifying moment, may lose control of our bladder and bowels and soil ourselves on the spot. Fear-pooping is the animal equivalent of an "oh, shit" moment.

Dead center on the welcome mat of the Westin Hotel, Aqutaq squatted and dropped a stinky load, much to my horror, that of my wife, and the less-than-amused expressions of the hotel staff and guests. It was mortifying, to say the least, but also predictable and avoidable.

Above, Aqutaq just days after her "oh, shit!" moment feeling more at ease in an environment better suited to her natural fear of novel situations; "neophobia."

Stop the Fear Before It Starts

While trainers like me try to plan for every eventuality, sometimes things escape our expectations, and we are met with an unwelcome surprise. But you can avoid this embarrassing fate. Luckily for domestic dog owners, the period by which neophobia sets in is dramatically longer, and the neophobic response is significantly blunted in most breeds of domestic dogs.[9] Even so, you can go a long way toward socializing your puppy by following the example of professional animal handlers. Simply employing the same protocol I use to desensitize young animals to as many stimuli as possible pays huge dividends for the rest of your animal's life.

But what if you have an older animal exhibiting fearfulness in certain situations? And what does fear look like, to begin with?

Some of the things you can look for are obvious. Are your dog's ears flat against its head? Is her tail tucked up under her belly? Is your dog yawning, licking its lips, or looking about with what humans might think is an expression of concern? Is your food-motivated dog disinterested in treats? All of these behaviors are indications your dog is anxious or afraid.

I have tricks for these circumstances, too. The first is to avoid overwhelming your animal and flooding them with fear and **adrenaline,** like I mistakenly did with Aqutaq at the fancy hotel. A terrified animal isn't going to learn anything, and excessive fear leads to ongoing, **traumatic** results. One of the mistakes I see people make most often with fearful animals is an attempt to force them through the frightening experience, rather than giving the animal a chance to understand what's happening and learn that the threat isn't as big as they imagine.

If your dog is resisting something, especially if they're on a leash, don't drag them into what they're scared of. That will do far more harm than good. While some people believe that humans should "face their fears," dogs need to attenuate them by understanding that they're not in any danger. Giving your dog the time and space they need to understand the new stimulus, or even pairing something positive, like a favorite treat, with exposure to the fear-inducing object or situation, can go a long way towards reducing that fear and gradually helping your dog to overcome whatever is causing them concern.

9   https://pmc.ncbi.nlm.nih.gov/articles/PMC2610618/#:~:text=Records%20of%20bites%20to%20111,dogs%20to%20obedience%20training%20classes

Flight Distance

It is crucial to give dogs time to attenuate to unfamiliar circumstances and redirect their behavior to form positive associations with what are initially fear-inducing moments. In wild wolves, there's something we call "flight distance." In the contemporary dog training world, this is often referred to as threshold or threshold distance, but since I'm talking about wolves and the animals I'm working with, I'll stick with the term flight distance for convenience.

The flight distance is the amount of ground an animal will cover to regain comfort when faced with something novel and scary. Flight distance might be 20 feet, 20 yards, or two miles, depending upon the source of the fear and what it takes to get far enough away that the animal no longer feels at risk.

With captive wolves or wolfdogs, I like to give flight distance too. If the animal is loose in a habitat, the flight distance is however far away they want to get, limited by the habitat fence. Out of habitat, on long lines, the flight distance is whatever the animal retreats to with me following their lead. You'll know an animal has reached their flight distance when they pause and look back. They're telling you in no uncertain terms, "Okay, I'm good here for a moment. I will evaluate the source of my fear and determine whether I need more distance, whether I'm comfortable where I am, or whether I might turn back now and begin a more measured investigation." For a video that showcases our approach to flight distance to blunt a neophobic response please check out: https://youtu.be/k35Dqd9fkBE?si=n7zkLig7K_VmorRp.

When your animals are afraid of something, follow their lead. Let them make as much space as they need. If they're leashed, as my animals always are when I take them on an out-of-habitat-patrol, you should maintain control of the situation by giving them the ability to retreat with you from whatever is causing them anxiety. Don't force your animals to face their fear. This treatment is akin to the old-school aversive or "balanced" training approach that, in my opinion, is unkind and often creates more problems than it resolves. What you'll do is reaffirm their fear to the point where it may be something you can never overcome, worse, by forcing your animals into over-threshold anxiety-provoking situations, you can damage the trust your animals have in you which is something that may be difficult, or even impossible to overcome. When your animals retreat, this is an ideal time to reassure them with calming words, or even positive contact. I often talk my animals through these situations with words like, "It's okay, you're okay, we don't care."

Why My Animals Love the Vet

But better than accommodating your animal in fear-inducing situations, anticipate those situations and work to familiarize the animal with the circumstance so it never gets scared in the first place. One of the most common instances where you'll see this is watching some poor person try to drag their terrified animal through the doors of a veterinarian's office. Veterinarian offices are typically one of the most horrifying places for our canine companions. It's pretty rare that a veterinary visit is a pleasurable experience for anyone's furred family member.

From a canine standpoint, it's an unfamiliar no man's land with unusual smells, unfamiliar people, the sounds of other animals in anguish, and instruments and hands handling them in ways they do not enjoy or condone.

But not my animals. They love going to the vet. To them, the veterinarian is a place where there are treats around every corner and friends waiting to greet them with open arms. It's no fun trying to get a 150-pound wolf through the vet door if they don't want to go there, and it's dangerous for technicians and even handlers to attempt to deal with a terrified and fear-aggressive animal because of the handler's incompetence.

So, how do I solve this problem? Most people only go to the vet when they have to, but not us. We go to the vet for fun a couple of times a month while our pups are in their pre-neophobic stage. We go to the vet's office to get treats, get pets, get weighed, and be handled by strangers, helping to make these activities fun and familiar instead of frightening.

During these visits, I gently introduce our animals to some of the tools of the trade. Thermometers and stethoscopes aren't nearly so terrifying when coupled with the friendly association of nice people and yummy treats. Sure, it's a big commitment, but the dividends are massive.

Wolves that don't benefit from this desensitization treatment during the first few months of their lives may have to be tranquilized before they're transported, which costs their caretakers thousands of dollars and exposes the animals to substantial risk since tranquilization is not without peril.

A social visit with Doctor Spears, our remarkable veterinarian. Bringing our pups for rewarding, low-stress vet visits pay huge dividends later on when the animals are big and powerful.

If you want to do right by your canine companion, my Wolfy Wisdom is simple: brief your vet on your objective. They won't mind, though they may charge you a few bucks for the visits. Even if they do, spend the money. It'll be one of the best investments you've made to guarantee that when your animal needs life-saving medical care, you'll have the best potential outcome. Another thing all new puppy parents should also try is to handle your dog in a manner similar to how your vet must, including handling their feet, palpating their bellies, examining their ears, and even the inside of their mouths. The more regularly you engage in these "mock exams," the better your pup will respond when the vet does the same thing.

After all, your dog is at ease, allowing the technicians and the veterinarian to do their best work without fear of being bitten, without the need to aggressively restrain an animal, and without the owner panicking because the animal is panicking, which creates a vicious cycle of fear and resistance.

If you use multiple vets, you should do a round-robin. If you have a vet who isn't interested in accommodating these requests, the solution is simple: find a different one. They're not the one for you.

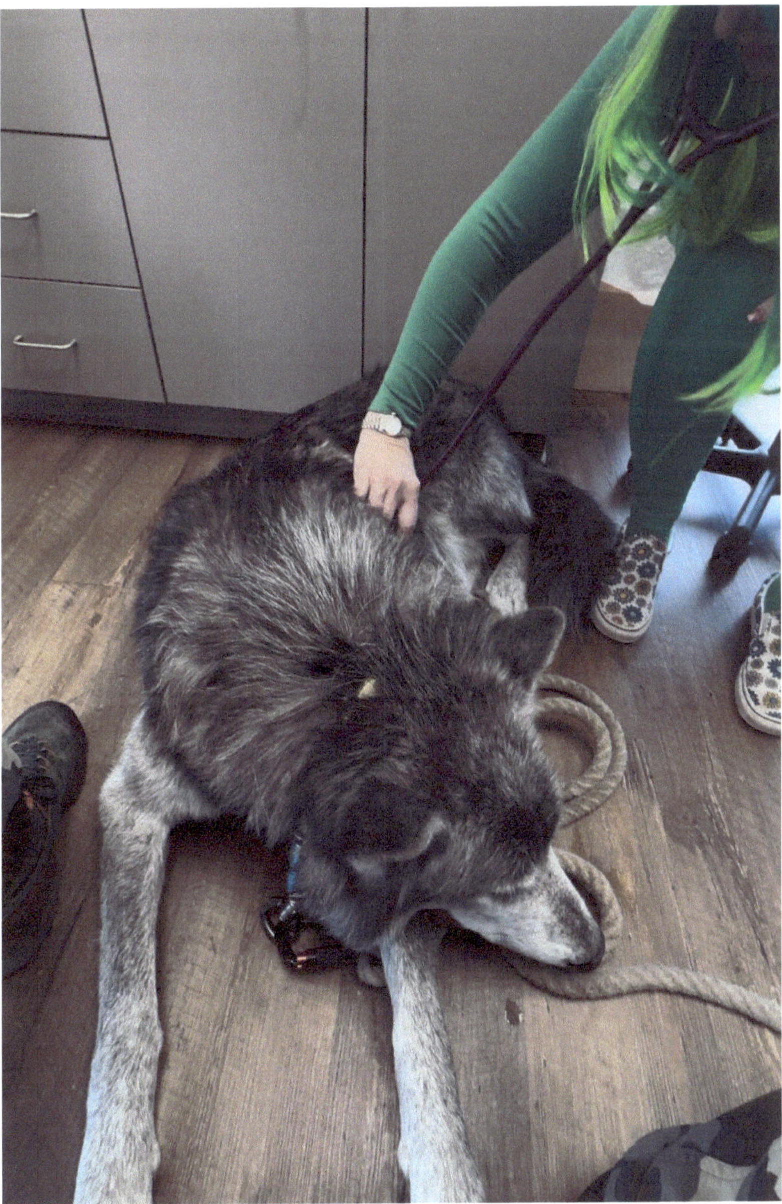

Dividends! Here, Iqniq is so at ease with our vet that even while she's decked out for Halloween, he's relaxed enough to snooze while the doctor places a stethoscope during a routine exam.

Here Are the Tricks of the Trade to Keep Your Canine Companion in Their Comfort Zone

- Introduce as many novel stimuli as possible early in your animal's life. This exposure should include music, appliances, unfamiliar people, different vehicles, garbage cans, big plastic bags, your veterinarian's office, hotels, tents, travel trailers, and anything else you can think of that will figure in your life with your dog.

- Never force your animal to "face their fears." This conditioning doesn't work and will create **trauma** that will be even harder to overcome, and it could potentially break the trust your animal has for you which is a catastrophic outcome that can permanently damage your relationship with your dog

- Understand the flight distance and allow your animal to exercise his or her discretion in what this distance should be.

- Pair positive reinforcement with fear-inducing stimulus to overcome any fear-inducing situation through patience and anxiety-reducing distractions.

- Be accepting. Some dogs will remain terrified of things or situations for no discernable reason. Our Giant Malamute, Bixby, clearly had a horrible puppy experience with a stack of boxes overhead. Despite being rock solid in every other aspect of his life, a big box in an overhead position was a non-starter for our boy. By identifying your dog's phobias, you can work around them to limit these negative environmental stimuli to your and your canine's benefit.

Not inmates! Sunny and Moonie share a pup cup of frozen yogurt during a short road trip to keep them used to riding in the wolfmobile.

Chapter 7:

Raise Teammates, not Inmates

You Don't See Wolves in the Circus

There's a saying I love about wolves: ***"Lions may be the king of the beasts, but you don't see wolves in the circus."***

This statement is generally true, but why is it? Certainly, lions are much more dangerous to humans than wolves are. Wild lions routinely kill people, and even captive lions have killed their handlers. So why is it that you see lions in the circus, but not wolves?

One reason is strategy. A lion might get mad and attack you, but it probably isn't actively plotting your demise. Wolves, as opportunistic hunters, may not challenge you directly, even if they detest you, but instead will wait for an opportunity, and when you least expect it, they'll get you good. Ask anyone who's worked with wolves for any length of time; we all have stories of being chewed up. Because of this tendency, people who are good with wolves understand that working with wolves is a collaboration, not a domination.

Collaboration, not Domination

This perspective goes with the "there's no alpha" concept, but it takes this one step further. With my family and our animals, we see them as full-fledged, autonomous family members. In other words, they're our teammates, not our inmates. But what does this mean in practice?

First and foremost, it means they have a say in what's happening to and with them. I don't force our animals to do something. The only exception is in some emergency circumstances, like a fire evacuation or emergency medical incident. But short of that, our animals get to make most of their life choices for themselves. If they want to be outside, I don't drag them in. If they want to be indoors, just like anyone in your house, they must follow a few rules. In my case, our animals are allowed to be inside so long as they're not actively destroying our furniture.

To be fair, there are times when our attention has strayed and our decor receives a "wolf haircut." At one time, I had nice furnishings. Now, I have formerly nice furnishings held together with duct tape and covered with moving blankets. It's not the classiest home in our area, but it is undoubtedly the "wolfiest," which suits us just fine!

But it goes beyond this as well. These are highly intelligent animals, just as dogs are. They have their own identity and sense of self and deserve to be treated respectfully like fellow sentient beings. The most important aspect of this relationship is understanding that your canine companion is your partner, not your plaything. Paying attention to your animal will give you great insight into what they want or don't want to do. And within reason, acceding to their wants will provide you with a much better relationship with your dog.

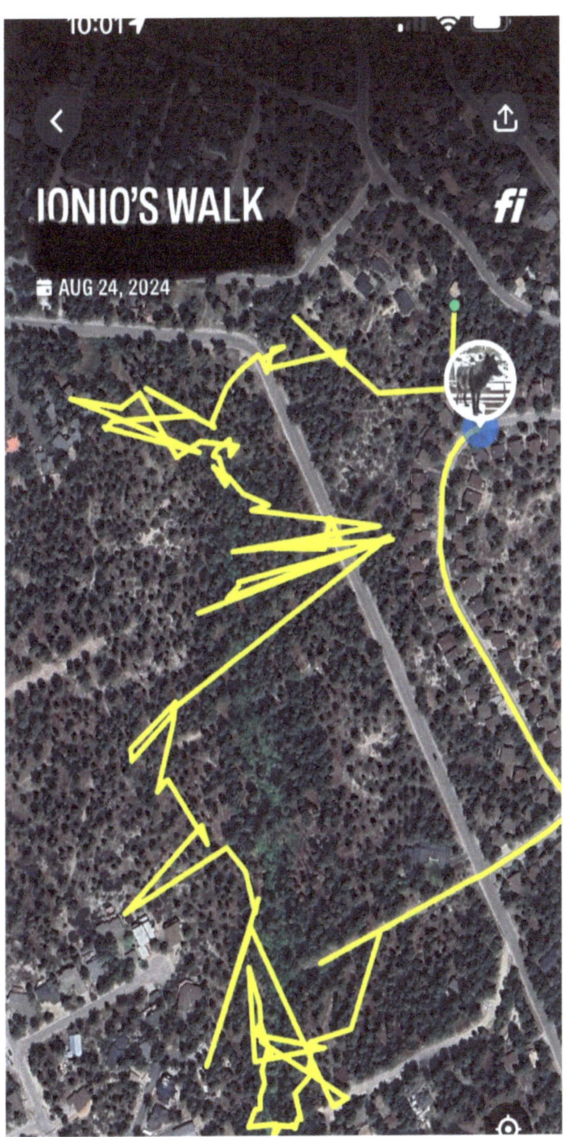

Iqniq's Meandering Patrol. It's definitely not a walk a human selected, but much more interesting for a canine.

Meandering Routes Through Swamps and Hedges

Nothing is sadder than watching somebody take their dog for a walk where the leash is taut because the owner is muscling the animal around. Often, as I'm dictating much of this book before putting it onto paper, I'm spending that time out with my animals. Today, as I'm working on this chapter, I'm out with Nunarjuaq, and we're walking in circles because that's what he wants to do. I track every walk I take, and you'd be amazed at the meandering routes that result from my animals deciding what's interesting and where they want to go.

Contrast this with the routes most people take with their dogs, which show a human objective, not a canine one, guiding the activity. In a subsequent chapter, I'll talk a lot more about walks and what to and not to do, but treating your animal like a teammate means letting them take charge and lead occasionally. Your job is to keep them out of trouble, not to control their every movement.

The bonus of treating your dog like a teammate and not an inmate is they'll express much more of their personality, and you'll understand your critter much more deeply. Just by giving my animals free lead on hikes, I've made incredible discoveries as they have found things that were interesting that I never would have noticed had I been the one taking charge. Just at this moment, I'm watching Nuni's fuzzy butt as he tries to crawl through a hedge. I'm not sure what's in there, but it's something that he finds attractive.

As I carry this to the extreme, some of my hikes are unpleasant when they drag me through swamps, thorny brush, and other places that humans tend to be less inclined to go. But that's okay. My walk is for my animal, not for me. I'm just along for the ride and to keep my furry people out of trouble.

Rock Hopping. Nunarjuaq, leading me on the path of most resistance.

Of all the chapters in this book, this one is the shortest and the easiest to apply. Just give your animals the freedom to be who and what they are; their personalities will blossom, and the relationship you share with them will be immeasurably deepened.

So what's the Wolfy Wisdom here? Wolves are individuals with unique personalities, and dogs are too. Let your dog be all who they want to be, and appreciate the uniqueness of every individual canine.

A strong relationship and continued preferential treatment of your original dog will pay big dividends with additional canine family members. Here, Bixby waits patiently knowing he's always first in line.

Chapter 8

Original Dog First

What We Can Learn From Wolves Fighting Wolves

As someone who has devoted his life to understanding wolves, you probably won't be surprised to learn that I spend much time reading scientific research. But a few years ago, a study was released that both blew my mind, opened my eyes to new possibilities, and was also a little bit heartbreaking. Kira Cassidy and fellow researchers at the Yellowstone Wolf Project conducted the study: "Battles Between Wolf Packs: How Nature and Nurture Influence Aggression."[10]

As I've mentioned before, wolves are very territorial. Aside from humans killing them, the most common cause of wolf mortality is wolf-on-wolf conflict. In Yellowstone National Park, where many wolves have telemetry collars, and it is relatively easy to observe them, especially in the winter, Kira cataloged over 400 different conflicts and potential conflicts, and developed a matrix that helped her predict when conflict would occur and what the outcome of that conflict would be.

---

10   https://academic.oup.com/beheco/article/26/5/1352/242442

After observing over 400 interactions, she developed a fascinating matrix. She assigned a point value to specific groups of animals, such as mature male wolves, mature female wolves, juvenile wolves of either sex, and wolves of great age. By adding up the totals on each side of a potential conflict, she was able to predict whether wolves would engage in conflict and, if they did engage, what the likely outcome of the conflict would be.

It's no surprise that wolf packs with lots of mature males tended to be more inclined to fight with neighboring packs and that if the pack had more mature males, they were more likely to win. With one fascinating proviso, wolves over eight years old, or ancient wolves, were worth two males of mature age, regardless of whether the old wolf was a male or a female.[11] As somebody who has studied wolves for a lifetime, I find the value of these ancient animals shocking. I always suspected there was deep cultural information contained in the heads of pack elders, but until I read this study, I didn't realize just how important the wisdom of older wolves was for the survival of a wolf family group. It was also heartbreaking because these old wolves are rare, especially in persecuted wolf populations.

The Vital Importance of Old Wolves

Why were the old wolves so important?[12] Clearly, they weren't the ones that were going to decide the outcome of a battle. A five or three-year-old wolf will almost invariably be more than a match for an eight-year-old wolf, a very old wild animal. So why? What makes old wolves so important? It turns out that the value of old wolves is experience. They're the generals commanding the armies and they understand better than the young testosterone-filled juveniles when to fight, when to retreat, and what to do when conflict occurs.

So what does this have to do with your canine companions? More than you might think. Nothing makes me sadder than seeing senior dogs at the pound. A dog that's devoted its whole life to its family only to be kicked to the curb when they become inconvenient due to health or expense, or even

---

11   It's important to know that while captive wolves can live up to 20 years, with 13 to 14 being typical, wild wolves, especially in areas where they are hunted, sustain very high mortality, with few wolves living five years and even fewer making it to eight. The oldest wild wolves on record, in protected areas like national parks almost never make it beyond 12 years of age.

12   For wolves, animals under a year are pups, those between their first and second year are yearlings, after a wolf's third winter they're adults, and animals older than five would be considered mature adults.

worse, because the family exchanged the old animal for a new puppy.

Frequently, older animals surrendered to the pound come with a litany of complaints about their behavior. But if an animal was perfectly acceptable for the first nine years of its life, then what changed to cause the behavior to become so undesirable as to merit a death sentence at the end? I've looked into this issue a lot and here's what I discovered.

Senior dogs know how to push your buttons.

Why Your Senior Dog "Goes Bad"

Canines view their humans as the ultimate remote control for everything good in their lives. And by the time a dog is a senior, they have figured out how to push your buttons and get what they need. You know them and they know you. And the relationship is generally pretty stable. But then, for whatever reason, a new dog is added to the equation and everything starts to go sideways. Oftentimes, frequently at the prodding of children, a puppy is added. And now the senior dog, who used to be the focus of the family's love and attention, finds itself displaced and neglected as the novelty of a puppy takes over.

So what happens then? In many cases, the senior dog, who's used to having a very functional remote control, suddenly finds itself outside of the attention and being rebuffed when they attempt to get what they were used to previously. And the thing is that sometimes the attention a puppy gets stimulates bad behavior on the part of the senior dog. They'll do anything to get attention if they need it. If the puppy is peeing on the carpet and everybody pays attention to it, the senior dog will figure out that if it pees on the carpet, it'll get attention. Of course, it's not the kind of attention that anybody wants to give.

The solution to this problem is so simple that I'm amazed no one has ever brought it to the forefront. And I sum it up as, the Original Dog first—meaning that whatever dog you had previously, regardless of their respective ages, is your "OD."

Our situation with our animals is unique. I currently have four age generations on our property, all interacting at the same time. But my protocol is quite simple. Whoever the most senior animal is that approaches and solicits attention gets priority. If a pup is climbing all over me and the matriarch comes over to say hi, I immediately refocus my attention to the more senior animal in our family hierarchy. This practice prevents the more mature animals from being needy or jealous. And puppies don't know any different. In the wild, just like in a human family, the youngest animals are at the bottom of the family pecking order, and it should be the same in your household.

When handing out treats, the senior dogs have priority. When handing out pets, same deal. Lavish love on the mature animals, and they won't need nearly so much because they won't feel threatened by the newcomer. You'd be amazed at what a massive difference this simple shift in thinking can make for households that add additional animals over time. And the best part of it is that your senior, who deserves all the love and attention in the world, won't find itself on the outside of the patio door looking in while being supplanted by a misbehaving, rude little pup that should be at the bottom of the order, not at the top.

When we add a new family member, like our puppy, Nepenthe, who joined our family to fill the void left by the passing of Bixby, our one domestic dog, we adhere strictly to our "Original Dog First" mantra. Not only does this help us avoid the onset of challenging behaviors and the development of jealousy from our older animals, but it also allows us to leverage the cultural wisdom of previous family members to indoctrinate the newcomers into our collective lifestyle.

Bixby, the OD (Original Dog) in the current family group along with a four-week-old Aqutaq.

The Wise Ways of Your Senior Dog

People shoot themselves in the foot when they ignore and bail on their aged dog. A dog who has adapted to your family's lifestyle is a cultural reservoir[13,14] of expert canine knowledge. But what do I mean by canine culture?

13   https://link.springer.com/content/pdf/10.3758/s13420-019-00400-w.pdf
14   https://www.nature.com/articles/s41599-020-0515-3

This topic is so vast, interesting, and important that it deserves a book of its own—one I may very well write next! But for people who may be unfamiliar with this idea, I define canine culture as knowledge and behavior that is transmitted from one dog to another—in other words, behavior that has been taught or learned and subsequently adopted by other animals in the same group, pack, family, or household.

Sometimes, these behaviors may exist in your family without you being aware of them until someone points them out. Perhaps you have dogs you've never trained who nevertheless perform various behaviors that you trained in your original dog but not subsequent canine family members.

For me, some cultural behavior among my animals is subtle. For example, we routinely pass beneath a ski gondola on our patrols. This circumstance doesn't seem to elicit a fear response for dogs, but it can be quite a frightening stimulus for wolves. I have found that when one of my wolves is paired with a domestic dog as we approach the gondola, the wolves observe the dog's response, and because the dog does not show anxiety, this reduces the wolf's fearfulness.

Subsequent regular exposure to the gondola where the dog leads helps desensitize the wolf to the situation. Once a wolf has been fully desensitized, that animal can be paired with another wolf who is naive to the gondola, and we can leverage the behavior of the now confident animal to indoctrinate the fearful one to become inured to the machine.

The same basic tenets apply to behaviors in the house. A naive dog will learn by observing an experienced conspecific. Getting rid of your dog who knows the ropes or consigning your older dog to a backyard jail because it "doesn't like the puppy" is, to put it bluntly, mean and ignorant.

Wolves know how to raise puppies. So do dogs. Unless you have a dog that is so territorial about your home that it's a danger to others, you should allow your more senior animal the opportunity to help you indoctrinate any newcomer into the "house rules."

Believe me when I tell you, any dog who has coexisted with your family for years knows every rule a new non-human family member should follow. Why would you want to spend all your time educating a new pup when your existing dog has the knowledge, the experience, and the tools to do so much of the job for you?

I've always leveraged the skills of a "mentor dog" to help us with our wolves. Our Giant Malamute, Bixby, who recently passed at fourteen, was the Sheriff inside our home–gently correcting misbehaving wolves or "wooing" (which is a sound malamutes make to get attention) his displeasure at unauthorized puppy activities to call them to our attention.

After he passed, we added a malamute puppy, Nepenthe to our family. Unfortunately, without Bixby's well-behaved presence, she's inherited the culture of our wolfy family members, leading to a delightful, but somewhat unruly personality that ultimately led me to author a children's book; *The Little Malamute Raised by Wolves*, that is available on multiple platforms as well as directly from my website: malamuteraisedbywolves.com

So what's the Wolfy Wisdom here? Everyone's the boss of the puppies, and just like the youngest children in a human family, they're at the bottom of the order.

- Do leverage your original dog to help educate your new family members in your house rules.

- Prioritize your older dogs' interactions, treats, and love.

- Don't ignore your more senior animals. They're your partners in this. Puppies are supposed to be at the bottom of the family pecking order. Elevating them in status creates resentment, will bring about jealousy, hostility, and possibly bad behavior in your otherwise well-behaved senior dogs, and violates the natural order of things in the canine world. A puppy SHOULD be at the bottom of the order. They'll get their turn at the top when they become more senior.

By following this simple Wolfy Wisdom, your original dogs will help you train your new animals, and they'll remain confident and well-behaved for the rest of their lives. When your older dogs cross over, the pups will be the ones to get priority.

A secure senior - your secret sauce for subsequent success. Here a 13-year-old Bixby still smiling and still ruling the house.

Iqniq's Umwelt - a world of ice and odor.

Part 2:

The Wolf Lifestyle: Umwelt

In the second part of this book, we're shifting gears from a more developmentally focused approach to the lifestyle you can create for yourself and your canine companies. Here, I'll talk about how canines experience the world and how you can leverage their different world experiences to improve the quality of their lives and perhaps open your own eyes and mind to how non-humans interact with their environment.

But first, I'll define for you that weird word up above; **umwelt.** This term, from biology, refers to the subjective world experienced by an organism; the way an animal perceives its environment. For example, an individual with a loss of vision has a dramatically different umwelt than sighted people. And of course, dogs and wolves have a decidedly different experience of the world than we do.[15]

---

15   https://pmc.ncbi.nlm.nih.gov/articles/PMC6199898/

Iqniq and Siqiniq engaging "jaw-sparring," a typical wolf behavior.

Chapter 9:

Wolves See the World Through Their Noses

Among terrestrial mammals, wolves have one of planet Earth's most acute senses of smell or olfaction. Their ability to pick up scents out of the air or on the ground exceeds even the extraordinary olfactory capabilities of bloodhounds. It's interesting to note that the olfactory nerves in canine brains are surprisingly close to their visual cortex.[16] To me, this anatomical arrangement speaks volumes. I believe that wolves literally see the world through their noses. But what does this mean?

There's a phenomenon known as synesthesia, where senses get mixed up. Sometimes, psychedelic drugs will elicit this effect where people believe that they see music or hear colors. But in the case of wolves, I suspect they see odors. For years, I tried to explain what I thought this would look like from a wolf's perspective, and then, one day, an artist did something magical. In the extraordinary animated film *Wolfwalkers*, there's a scene and a music video called *Running with the Wolves Tonight* where a young girl magically transforms into a wolf. The artist has accomplished something I've never been able to convey through my words. The animator shows the world through the eyes and nose of the animated wolves. Odors pour off of different things in streams of sparkling color. Puddles exude their own odor. Other animals do as well. It is a magical representation of what wolves

---

16   https://pmc.ncbi.nlm.nih.gov/articles/PMC10216273/

perceive every day of their lives.

The manifestation of this capability is something to behold. As part of my routine with our animals, I give them tremendous latitude when we go out on our regular patrols. This approach means they're free to explore what they find interesting. If they pick up an interesting scent trail, they're free to follow it with me on the other end of their long line. One day in particular illustrated to me just how remarkable a wolf's nose really is.

I was out with my female wolf, Aqutaq, on a hike in the Sierras, and it was clear to me that she had picked up something interesting in the air. She was tracking in a specific direction for a very long time, pausing occasionally to taste the air with her mouth open and strong inhalations. Even though she was taking me quite a bit further than I intended, I was curious about what captured her attention, that she was taking a very unfamiliar route. Five miles, six miles, seven miles, she was still air-sensing something that had her transfixed. Then we came over a small ridge, and below us was a herd of deer in a meadow, something highly unusual in our area. If I hadn't seen it for myself, there's no way I'd believe that a wolf could smell something seven miles away, but she had, and she did.

In my opinion, this is how wolves might see their world.

The idea that their capabilities are so advanced was a real awakening to me, and it helped me understand even better just how primary a wolf's sense of smell is in helping it to navigate its environment, figure out who's there, and most importantly, find its next meal. While our domestic canine companions may not have a sense of smell quite as developed as wolves, their olfactory capabilities are still extraordinary, extending even to specialized skills, including detecting cancer, drugs, money, and even the onset of arrhythmias and seizures.[17,18] Recognizing the primary importance of olfaction in our pets goes a long way to understanding their cognition and helping us improve their lives and, thus, our own.

In prior chapters, you'll recall how much I leverage olfaction, particularly at the developmental stages of our pups. However, understanding the primary importance of smell throughout your dog's life is critical, too. Dogs process a tremendous amount of information through their noses, but you have to give them the freedom to do it; when taking your dog for a walk, you need to let them sniff as deeply and as long as they'd like. Just because what they're sniffing appears uninteresting to you doesn't mean it's boring to them at all.

Your Dog Sees the World Through Its Nose, Too

Finally, understanding the exquisite olfactory capabilities of your pet should inform you about things in your home. All of us have encountered somebody who wears too much perfume or cologne or the cloying scent of an overabundant potpourri in someone's home. Now imagine your sense of smell is 10,000 times better, and consider what those insults would do to your brain. Our modern homes are filled with things that generate olfactory overload for dogs: scented candles, Glade plug-ins, dryer sheets, Febreze, personal care products, and the list goes on. Polluting your home with these odorous toxicants is, at best, unpleasant for your dog and, at worst, can cause them harm. It's not that great for us, either. If you can smell it, it means you're inhaling chemicals. And if you can smell it, they can smell it from miles away.

Our practice in the home is to eliminate every one of these noxious chemical cover-ups to the greatest extent possible. We don't use dryer sheets,

---

17   https://www.ncbi.nlm.nih.gov/pmc/articles/PMC4859551/
18   https://www.ncbi.nlm.nih.gov/pmc/articles/PMC9106054/

scented detergents, scented candles, cologne, perfume, or any personal care products with strong odors. If you can smell your house from outside, you know you've created a noxious indoor environment for the exquisitely tuned canine sense of smell. Give your dog's nose and lungs a break as well. In the modern world, our bodies are assaulted with chemicals nonstop. Limiting exposure in the home for yourself and your animals will do you both a favor.

Olfactory treats can also be used as enrichment. Dogs love stinky stuff, but they can love pleasant-smelling stuff as well. One of our favorite things to do as an enrichment exercise for our animals is to spritz healthy and beneficial scents on things for them to scent roll. Scent rolling is a behavior that I call the wolf equivalent of trying on a new perfume. If you're unlucky, that perfume could be bear poop. Still, by planning ahead, you can leverage their desire to wear novel fragrances by using things like all-natural essential oils that have the added benefit of deterring pests from infesting your pet. Our animals particularly like a product used to wash plants, which also removes the smell of urine called Tweetmint. It's got botanical extracts that smell wonderful, and our animals can't resist it. For wolves, it's a little like catnip. I can spray it on a surface, and they'll roll around in delight. You can do the same thing for your pups, and they'll smell better and be delighted that you gave them an olfactory treat.[19]

So what are my words of Wolfy Wisdom on seeing the world through your animal's eyes? Remember their noses. They're every bit as important. Do remove all heavily scented sources of odor in your home. You may like the scent, but remember, at 10,000 times the potency, it probably isn't good for your dog. Remember that smelling their world is every bit as important in their explorations as seeing it. Let them lead the walk with their nose if that's their inclination. Finally, use interesting smells as enrichment. Buy things your animals can't resist that are also beneficial for them and apply them to towels, furniture, or other surfaces your dog might want to rub against. They'll smell delicious and be happier canines if you do this regularly.

---

19   If you want to go even deeper down the enrichment path, this book is a great inspiration: https://www.amazon.com/Canine-Enrichment-Real-World-Making/dp/1617812684/ref=sr_1_1?sr=8-1

Moonie scents something suspicious. Photo by Scott Bye.

Iqniq pushing me and my MSR snowshoes during a patrol in December 2022.

Chapter 10:

Patrols, Not Walks

I love fuzzy butts, and it's a good thing because I spend hours a day staring at the fuzzy butt of one or more of my animals as they lead me on a daily patrol. You'll notice I said patrol, not walk. There's a difference: allow me to explain.

Wolves Post "No-Trespassing" Signs

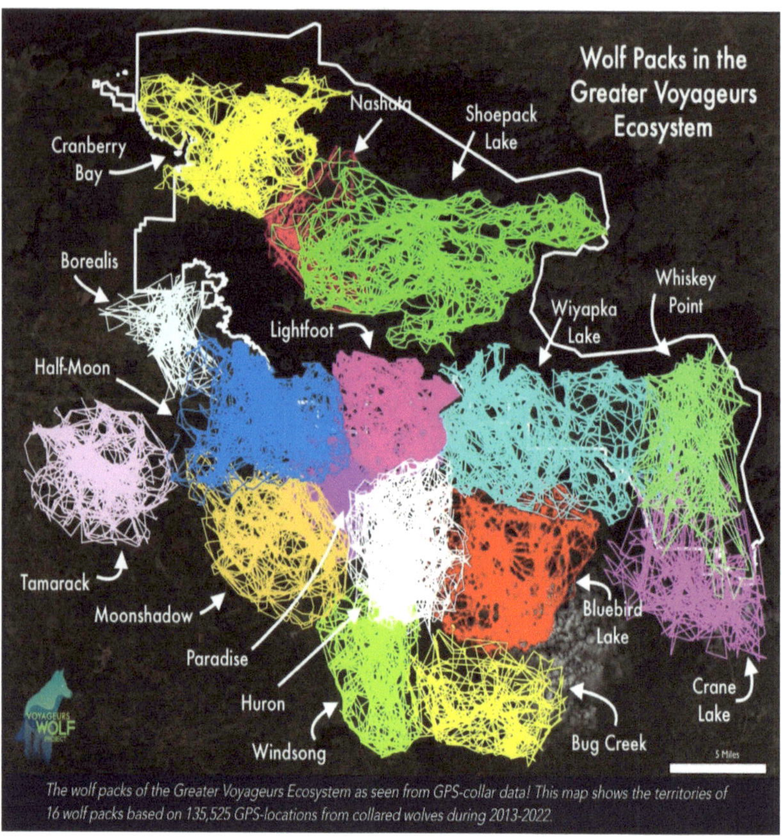

The wolf packs of the Greater Voyageurs Ecosystem as seen from GPS-collar data! This map shows the territories of 16 wolf packs based on 135,525 GPS-locations from collared wolves during 2013-2022.

But first, let's talk about wild wolves. Most wild wolf families maintain a very specific territory. The size of that territory can vary enormously, from wolves in Minnesota with territories as small as 70 square miles, which is what you see in the image above (generated by the Voyageurs Wolf Project using almost a decade of telemetry collar data), to wolves in the high Arctic with territories encompassing thousands of square miles as they follow nomadic prey populations.

But for our purposes, I'm going to talk about wolves that keep relatively small territories, such as the wolves in Yellowstone National Park, which is situated mostly within Wyoming but also extends into Idaho and Montana, or the wolves in the Voyagers ecosystem in the Boundary Waters wilderness area in Northern Minnesota.

We know a lot about the territories of these wolves because they have radio telemetry collars that allow us to plot where the wolves go over time. These plots give us incredibly accurate polygons showing the territories of various wolf families. So specific are the boundaries these wolves enforce that when you view the plots, it looks like they fence themselves in or out.

Typically, within these territories, wolves will spend considerable time patrolling the boundaries that are adjacent to other family groups. The majority of scent marking, scraping, and scat placement in these areas is dedicated to posting "No Trespassing" signs. I like to say that dogs post messages and wolves post warnings. The difference is that dogs typically say, "I was here," when they tag a fire hydrant or a tree, while wolves say, "I am here; keep out."

Wolves are very serious about enforcing their territorial boundaries. Aside from attrition due to humans, the number one most common cause of death among wild wolves is conflict with other wolves, typically over territorial boundaries.[20],[21] A lone wolf, which is more accurately called a ***disperser***[22], might find itself in real trouble if it crosses into a wolf pack's territory and gets itself found out. Wolves can be pretty merciless when they encounter an intruder, and if the animal escapes with its life, it's lucky.

Rethinking the Walk by Letting Your Dog Lead

But how does this relate to what we do with our domestic dogs or even what I do with my wolf family? Firstly, I want you to rethink what a walk is about.

---

20   https://www.nps.gov/yell/learn/nature/wolves.htm
21   https://wolf.org/wp-content/uploads/2020/11/367-Seasonality-of-Intraspecific-mortality-by-gray-wolves.pdf
22   Dispersers, commonly called lone wolves, are wolves that have left their natal group in an effort to find a mate and unoccupied territory. This is one of the most dangerous times in a wolf's life as they leave the protection of their family, and they may encounter other, hostile wolves as they search for a partner and a place of their own. It's especially ironic that there's so much negative mythology associated with "lone wolves" since they're actually looking for love, not trouble.

All too often, I see people who take their dogs out principally to encourage them to relieve themselves. Frequently, these walks are limited to the same prescribed route, day after day, week after week, month after month. Now, if it's boring for you, imagine how sad and tedious it is for your canine, whose senses are much more developed than ours. A walk is something humans do. A patrol is something wolves do. Or as my brother said, "Dogs don't walk in straight lines; humans do."

A patrol is not a static activity, repeating the same route every time. When you look at the telemetry from wild wolves, you'll see the incredible variation in their movements, day over day.[23] Rethinking what it means to take your dog out on an excursion will transform the experience for you and your animal.

As I've said in prior chapters, canines are intelligent, self-aware, and have their own interests and desires; the problem for many dogs is that humans don't allow them to express them. Going out with your dog and letting them make the decisions is critical for their intellectual and psychological well-being. Instead of thinking of the walk as an activity that you guide, think of the patrol as an activity you follow, shepherd, and enjoy.

When I'm out with my wolves, my job is simple: keep them out of trouble and don't get hurt while following them. I've heard people call me the world's most extreme dog walker, and there's probably some truth to that, given the places my animals frequently wish to go. Your experience doesn't need to be nearly so extreme. But by considering what might be interesting to your animal and giving them the opportunity to explore, you'll learn new things about your dog, and every walk will become an adventure instead of an obligation.

---

23   Be sure to visit this link to see some extraordinary animations created from wolf collar telemetry and synthesized by the Voyageurs Wolf Project. https://www.voyageurswolfproject.org/animations

Fuzzy butts! My usual view on every patrol as the canines lead the charge.

Leveraging Patrols to Keep Your Canine Safe

But there's more to patrols than that. One of my great fears is that a tree could come down, take out a section of my fence, and result in animals loose on the landscape. While I spare no expense to maintain our habitat, remove hazardous trees, and use Fi tracking collars on every one of our animals with a geofence that gives us notifications, nothing is 100% certain. Therefore, I plan ahead for the eventuality of an escape.

So what does that look like? Well, I leverage the territorial behavior of my animals to help me create a secondary geofence of their own choosing. We have thousands of acres of wilderness out our door, but there are specific directions that entail more risk due to traffic, habitation, and the likelihood of my animals encountering other people or other dogs. To encourage them to never go in this direction, I never do. They've established a hard territorial boundary along one section of our route, and it is my belief, based upon their behavior and the behavior of wild wolves, that should they be loose on the landscape without my presence, the last place they go is the no man's land on the other side of their established territory.

You can do the same thing. Within the areas where you exercise your animals, determine your high-risk zones. Then be certain that with every patrol you conduct, your animals set up a boundary that you never transgress along that zone. By allowing them to scent mark and create their own natural geofence, it's possible to significantly limit their inclination to go beyond those areas if they happen to be loose without your presence.

Ideally, you'll identify areas that are especially safe, particularly from vehicular traffic or the possibility that your animals are going to run into something that could cause them bodily harm. Because I've taken years to establish this pattern, I believe that should the worst thing happen and an animal gets loose, they are going to stay within their naturally comfortable zone, giving me the greatest opportunity to use telemetry to locate them and get them back under my control.

Interestingly, my brother, who is himself a highly skilled dog parent and the former president of one of the oldest dog clubs in Los Angeles, related the following story to me, emphasizing how important it is to walk your dogs in the area where you live and to use my tips about establishing territorial boundaries to act as olfactory and psychological geofences for your dogs.

"Years ago we found a stray and immediately took her to the South LA Animal Shelter (now closed), to see if she had a microchip. While we were waiting an employee–a janitor–started chatting with us. Mind you, he was not an animal professional; he was just a hardworking guy who understood the various aspects of his job environment.

He said to us, "On any given night, we have over 400 dogs here, and EVERY ONE of them has a home. But their owners don't walk them, and because of that, they (the dogs) don't know their neighborhood. So, when they escape and are spooked by fireworks or a car backfiring, they run and can't find their way home."

"This reality has always resonated with me and been heartbreaking."

Wolves Hate Dog Parks

It's important to note that wolves hate dog parks. As I mentioned, wolves are incredibly territorial and tend to prefer to stay in familiar territory. While some dogs enjoy dog parks, not every dog does, and not every dog park is a good environment for a dog. Domestic canines are much more flexibly sociable than wolves. Wolves are a bit like Dexter the fictitious serial killer who in Episode 11, Season Three, says, "I don't get to have friends"; for the most part, wolves don't get to have friends either. Dogs, of course, do have friends. The one distinct behavioral difference between wolf family groups and feral dogs is that feral dogs frequently form loose associations with one another, where they are somewhat cooperative in their interactions in pursuit of food and defense. With wolves, the family is everything, and everyone not in the family is "other" and a potential threat.[24]

I recommend not considering dog parks part of a patrol. If your dog does happen to enjoy the dog park, there's nothing wrong with that, but do keep in mind that dog parks frequently stimulate unwanted behaviors, are a repository for disease, and, in many cases, an excuse for people to let go of the leash without engaging with their dog in any meaningful way. Needless to say, I am not a fan.

____

24　　https://womensanimalcenter.org/sites/default/files/documents/2018-09/Are%20Dogs%20Really%20Pack%20Animals.pdf

Using Urine to Establish Territory

Most people who dearly love wolves have seen the screenplay or read the book of Farley Mowat's "Never Cry Wolf." In it, there's a hilarious scene where the biologist is concerned about a wolf coming into his camp, and he elects to urinate around the perimeter of his abode to keep him out. In the movie, it's quite a hilarious scene, but in my life, it's a hilarious reality.

But it's not to keep things out. As anybody with dogs knows, they use urine to announce their presence and for wolves to establish territorial boundaries. But wolves also use urine to identify one another on the landscape and, perhaps even more importantly, to reaffirm social ties.

One behavior in particular is super interesting. It's called scent mark reinforcement or marking over. Typically, this behavior is engaged in by the breeding pair. If one animal urinates to create a scent post, the opposite sex partner will urinate on top of it, reinforcing the mark. The matriarch of our wolf family unit, Aqutaq, often reinforces my scent marks.

I'm a big fan of Edward Abbey, and I take to heart his statement that if you can't pee in your own front yard, you live too close to town. While my neighbors may have had an eyeful a time or two, my behavior is intended to establish and reaffirm our core territory. But what's funny is how frequently Aqutaq will come over and reinforce my scent mark. I'd call this a coincidence if this were just a one-time occurrence. But this happens consistently.

Your Aim Sucks! (or Not)

In fact, and this is a funny aside, I had an interesting discussion with my wife a few years ago. She was in our shared bathroom when she called me in and said, "Honey, I think we have a problem." She continued, "I think you're coming in here at night and peeing all over the toilet."

"No way," I said. "I have good aim and a toilet nightlight. It's not me."

She rolled her eyes and said, "Then why does it smell like pee in here?" I sniffed and agreed. It did smell like pee in our bathroom. But it wasn't the aroma of human urine. Instead, it was the pungent wild animal ammonia odor of wolf peeper. I explained to her how Aqutaq frequently reinforces my scent mark and suggested that perhaps while we were asleep, Aqu was getting up, going into the bathroom, and peeing in the place that smelled of my urine within the house. She laughed, said nice try, and told me I'd better work on my aim.

No sooner had she said the last when Aqutaq walked into the bathroom, looked at both of us, lifted her leg, and urinated all over the toilet, the cabinets, and the floor. "I'll take that hundred bucks now," I said to her.

So what's the point of this? Well, it's not a bad idea, provided you don't live in an apartment complex and have your own yard or if you're engaging in regular hikes with your canines to occasionally scent mark along with them. It's fun, it's funny, and your dog will feel that much closer to you for engaging in a shared and meaningful behavior.

So what's the Wolfy Wisdom for patrols? Simple: rethink your walk and turn it into a patrol. Let your canine lead at their pace and make decisions as to the route. Maintain gentle guidance as to where you go, and limit their ability to develop territories that incorporate dangerous places. Within the territory you establish, allow the animal to take varied routes, change directions, patrol at different times of the day, and generally give your dog an opportunity to make its life off your premises more interesting.

Peeper marks the spot! Yes, dominant females also engage in raised or flexed leg urination "FLUs." Here, Aqutaq is making sure to post ample "no-trespassing signs' during one of our regular patrols.

Wolfy Greeting. When wolves greet family, they want to lick their teeth. Here, Nunarjuaq and Aqutaq welcome me back after a day away.

Chapter 11:

You Let Your Dog Lick You Where?

Gross or Greeting?

Nothing I post online generates more mixed reactions than videos of my animals greeting me, especially those where they lick my face and even my mouth. Frequently, I get vomit-face emojis and disgusted comments, with people opining that their dogs lick themselves in unmentionable places and that it's gross that I would let my dogs lick my face or my mouth.

But I have a different opinion, informed by wolf behavior and decades of direct contact with wolves and primitive dogs. In the wild, you'll observe that wolves spend considerable time in each other's faces. Very young pups lick the mouths of every other wolf in their family, both as a greeting and, more importantly, as a means to get them to regurgitate food for the pups to eat. Even as the pups grow older and no longer require regurgitated food for sustenance, they'll still rush the older wolves in their family and greet them with a very puppy-like face-licking behavior. Then, as wolves get older, you'll note they regularly engage in a ritualized greeting of licking one another on the mouth. What they're actually doing is licking each other's teeth. Clearly, a tremendous amount of olfactory information is associated with an animal's mouth. In my opinion, canid mouths are the equivalent of human hands. They're the most dexterous and essential part of the animal's body and are the principal means of **tactilely** exploring their environment. Wolves licking one another's mouths is similar to a human handshake, only more intimate.

Refusing Is Rude

So when my animals greet me, I never rebuff their attempts to lick me in the face and, most particularly, to lick me in the mouth. I know that this is a social glue for our family group, and it maintains and deepens the bonds I share with my animals. In my opinion, and the opinion of my wolves, declining such a warm invitation would be rude and uncool. I don't do that. I also know that certain undesirable canine behaviors can be truncated by letting your dog lick you in the face or the mouth. Many dogs are going to try, and if you make it easy for them, not only will they love you more for it, but you'll also prevent things like animals from jumping up on you.

Why do wolves, wolf dogs, and dogs jump up? They're trying to get to your mouth. They're trying to greet you. They're trying to shake your hand. Humans have faces in a strange place compared to dogs, and dogs are doing their best to accommodate this difference by standing on their hind legs and trying to get close to your mouth to greet you as a family member or good friend. Instead of being frustrated that a dog is jumping up, accommodate the dog by kneeling. Give them a chance to greet you, and they'll be satisfied that they've said hello the proper canine way.

Now that you understand this, you'll have a much greater appreciation for your dog's desire to lick you in the face. You'll also notice this behavior among dogs that are friendly with one another. Especially if you're a student of wolves, you'll observe these behaviors in wild wolves, especially dynamic families with many generations of offspring.

Some people are concerned that dogs will have disgusting breath or, worse, that they might transmit some kind of illness to humans as a result of allowing their tongue near your mouth. While it is true that some dogs have gross breath, that tends to be a hygiene and feeding issue and is not a problem with the dog but with what you are doing or feeding. Never in the 40 years that I've had wolves have I had a wolf lick me in the mouth and been disgusted by what I tasted, and never in 40 years have I contracted an illness associated with that behavior. I don't believe there are any illnesses transmissible from dogs to humans via a lick, provided the animal has been vaccinated for rabies.

So what's the Wolfy Wisdom? Don't be rude to your canine. They love you and want to show it by a familial greeting. Grant them the opportunity. Make it easy for them by bending to their level instead of making them jump up to yours. And if you don't like your dog licking you in the face, my advice is to get used to it. If you want to love your dog and you want your dog to love you back, you need to adapt to the social niceties of canine family greetings.

Puppy kisses! Moonie solicits me for a snack while Sunny looks at the photographer.

"I thought we agreed, no wolves in the bed."

Chapter 12:

Let Your Dog on the Sofa and the Bed

One of my favorite cartoons shows a series of vignettes of a family with a new dog. At first, the dog isn't allowed on the sofa. Then it's allowed on the sofa but not the bed. Then it's allowed on the sofa and the bed. Before long, humans were only allowed to stay on the bed and the sofa as long as it didn't disturb the dog. I love this because I live this.

The Shabby Chic of Duct Tape and Moving Blankets

We used to have nice furniture. But now, thanks to "wolf haircuts," we have formerly nice furniture covered with moving blankets and duct tape. That's what it takes to accommodate our toothy canine family members. If you observe wolves in the wild, you'll notice that they like to share space. If it's particularly warm, they may not be touching, but you'll see that wolf family groups spend a lot of time in close proximity. And in cold conditions, they may sleep quite close to one another for shared warmth. But much like the face licking I mentioned in the previous chapter, laying close together en-hances social bonds and creates a sense of ease and comfort amongst family members. Another benefit of this close association is that studies show that the behavior stimulates the release of oxytocin for both humans and dogs.[25] For those unfamiliar with this hormone's benefits, oxytocin lowers stress and anxiety, builds trust, and fosters social connections. It may also influence mood and mental health.[26]

Of course, human homes are not the wilds that wolves enjoy. But to our dogs, this is their primary territory. It is the rendezvous site where the family meets, greets, eats, rests, and sleeps. In my experience, creating artificial exclusionary zones limits the intimacy you can enjoy with your canine. To me, having happy dogs is much more important than having beautiful furnishings. And I'm sure the canines with whom I share my life are much more inclined to damage my sofa than yours.

A dog may gnaw the arm of your sofa; a wolf will reduce it to feathers and splinters. And that's not much of an exaggeration.

---

25   https://pmc.ncbi.nlm.nih.gov/articles/PMC6826447/#:~:text=Simple%20Summary,linked%20to%20positive%20emotional%20states
26   https://pubmed.ncbi.nlm.nih.gov/15834840/

Nap time! Sharing the sofa with a very puppy Nunarjuaq.

High Spots and Peaky Places

In addition to the comfort and satisfaction of enjoying a bed or a sofa, there's a significant olfactory component as well. The places where you park yourself regularly will be the most deeply suffused with your scent, a scent that, to a canine, says family and home. Further, within any house, the furnishings and the beds tend to be the highest vantage points reasonably accessible to a dog. Canids like to look down on things from high. For this reason, I always incorporate platforms and other elevations in our habitats.

My wife and I have entirely customized our bedroom to accommodate our animals in my home. We've done this by cutting narrow windows that run up the wall at a diagonal so that from the bed, the animals have different secluded vantage points from which to examine the goings-on outside their secluded bedroom den. We've also built a platform immediately adjacent to our bed and contiguous with it so our canines can sleep with us without fully kicking us off our bed. Of course, most folks think we're crazy people. In the winter, when our animals have their full winter fur, we regularly keep our bedroom below 50 degrees so the animals aren't too hot at night, though I'm not suggesting you go to those lengths unless you really enjoy sleeping cold.

We customized it! Our bedroom during Aqutaq's birthday celebration. Note the unusual windows cut into the wall giving our animals the secluded peaky places mentioned.

So, what's the Wolfy Wisdom here? Get a bunch of old blankets (I use the high-quality moving blankets you can get from Harbor Freight or other similar stores) or other protective covers and become tolerant of a little dirt and muddy footprints on your couch, chairs, and bed. You'll save yourself the trouble of shooing your animals off the places they most want to be, and you'll benefit from the wonderful connection you get from having your dog sleep with you on a cold winter night.

The excitement is evident on Nepenthe's face as the two of us head off on an adventure. Nothing strengthens our bonds with our animals like including them in our lives as much as possible.

Chapter 13

Time Together: Wolves Hang Out With Their Families

If you've ever gone to Yellowstone and watched the wolves or enjoyed any true documentary about the species, you'll notice that wolves spend a lot of time hanging out. Like all supreme wilderness survivalists, wolves know not to waste much energy. When they're not eating, hunting, patrolling their territory boundaries, or playing with one another, wolves spend much time watching the world go by. And you'll notice that they do this near one another. Perhaps three out of seven wolves will be dozing while the other four are awake.

Sleeping With One Ear Open

Wolves sleep with one ear open during these periods. Not only do proximity and relaxation allow for better rest, but because there's always at least one animal on semi-alert, the others can let their guard down and recover. But more important is the simple congeniality of hanging out with your family. Wolves form incredibly close familial bonds, and they enjoy one another's company, studies even show that this close association stimulates the release of **oxytocin**, sometimes called the "love hormone."[27] The same holds true for the wolves in my care. You'll almost invariably find them all spread out just a little but situated near one another in any particular area of their habitat. If I go somewhere in the habitat and simply sit down, before long, first one, then the rest of the animals will relocate near where I am.

I intentionally live my life so I'm closely connected to my animals that they go where I go. And I do that a lot. I have constructed my life so that I can spend hours every day simply hanging out with my canines. And during that time, I don't do much. I'm not succumbing to the modern phenomena of TikTok brain, with my nose in my phone and my senses closed off from the outside world. On the contrary, this is my church, my meditation, and it's my greatest joy simply observing the world and my animals from the vantage points they prefer. It helps me maintain a deeper connection with nature and the animals I love.

---

27   In fact, many biologists have observed that few species share so many common social attributes as wolves and humans. Wolves, the ancestors of dogs, are one of the most cooperative canine species. This cooperative propensity derives from the fact that each subject needs other group members to obtain resources and increase survival. The pack functions as a unit in which each individual collaborates in territory defence, hunting, and rearing of offspring. For this reason, even though a clear hierarchy exists among wolves, subordinates can provide help to dominants to obtain social tolerance in a sort of commodity exchange. Wolves can make peace after aggression, console victims of a conflict, and calm down the aggressors. This set of behaviors, also called post-conflict strategies, requires a social attentiveness towards others' emotional state and the ability to coordinate appropriate reactions. Adult wolves also play. They engage in play fighting, which strongly resembles real fighting, by finely modulating their motor actions and quickly interpreting playmates' intentions, thus maintaining the non-serious playful mood. All these cognitive and social skills were a fertile ground for the artificial selection operated by humans to redirect the cooperative propensity of wolves towards dog–human affective relationship. https://pmc.ncbi.nlm.nih.gov/articles/PMC6912837/

How many canines do you count in this photo? Despite having a multi-acre habitat, we invariably find our animals relaxing near one another.

Contrast this with what I typically see with humans and their canine companions. Even when they're with their dogs, they're not really with their dogs. People use a dog park as a fenced-in babysitter, not a place to engage with their animals off the leash. And I'm not sure I've ever seen anyone but me simply sitting on the ground, hanging out with their canines, watching the world go by. But you should. Part of loving a dog is loving its umwelt[28], their world experience. And the best way to understand their world experience is to be an active participant in it.

If this is hard for you, consider it an exercise in mindfulness. Even 30 minutes with your phone shut off and your eyes and ears open to nature and the behavior of your animals will pay huge dividends, both for you and for your canine companions. And the things you'll learn will surprise you. Most people don't know the sounds that arouse interest in their dogs, or the sights, or the smells. But by observing your animals' behavior when you're simply hanging out, the lessons they teach you can be profound.

---

28   Umwelt is a German word that translates to "environment" or "surrounding world" in English. In the context of animal behavior and ethology, umwelt refers to the unique perceptual world experienced by a particular organism. It encompasses all the sensory inputs and experiences that an organism perceives and interacts with, essentially representing the subjective reality of that organism.

The term was coined by the biologist Jakob von Uexküll, who used it to describe how different animals have different perceptual worlds based on their sensory capabilities and ecological niches. For example, the umwelt of a dog includes smells and sounds that humans might not notice, while the umwelt of a bee includes ultraviolet patterns on flowers that humans cannot see.

In essence, umwelt highlights the idea that every species perceives the world differently, based on its own sensory and cognitive abilities, leading to a unique, species-specific experience of reality.

Here Are Your Wolfy Wisdom Cliff Notes for This Chapter:

🐾 Don't use dog parks as dog babysitters.

🐾 Being WITH your dog means sharing its umwelt (no phones!). Playing sudoku while sitting with your canine doesn't count!

🐾 Do spend time in your dog's world when they're resting but awake.

🐾 Treat your dog-centered time as an exercise in mindfulness. Try to understand what captures your dog's attention. By tuning into what your dog tunes into, you'll gain a greater understanding of your dog's senses, thoughts, and feelings.

Iqniq appreciates the high vantage points in his biologically appropriate habitat.

Chapter 14:

Habitats, not Prisons (Rethinking Your Yard for the Wolf in Your Dog)

The Heartbreaking Reality of Backyard Prisons

For many of us, seeing animals in a roadside zoo's sterile and unnatural environment is about as heartbreaking a thing as anyone who loves animals can witness. You can see the desperation in the eyes of those animals being held for a lifetime against their will in a wholly inappropriate and repugnant prison. Fortunately, modern zoological gardens do a much better job creating biologically appropriate habitats for their residents, particularly those meeting the stringent American Zoological Association standards.

Unfortunately, many of our domestic companions live in the equivalent of a zoo-like prison, only behind a fence where no one can see. In some cases this is actual neglect, but in many instances people simply don't know any better. Let's change this!

Individuals like me who work with wolfdogs and wolves understand the importance of a biologically appropriate, large habitat that provides the animals with an environment analogous to what they would enjoy were they free-living. I hate the word enclosure. An enclosure is synonymous with a prison, and the mindset is similar. An enclosure is intended to keep something in. A habitat, on the other hand, is something that supports a natural life experience.

Natural rock outcroppings provide habitat for small game and an opportunity for Sunny and Moonie to practice their rodent hunting skills.

My view of an appropriate habitat is perhaps the most extreme of anyone who does what I do, since my home is entirely within the living space I provide for our animals. What differentiates us from everyone else I'm aware of is our commitment to sharing our entire lives with our animals by having our home completely within our habitat. Because of our commitment to the social dynamics of our wolf family group, our situation is not without its challenges. I've lost our groceries running the gauntlet from our airlock to the front door more than once when I've gotten sloppy. And, of course, our home is a bit worse for wear. Two years ago, I had to nail copper plating to our front door because Iqniq was slowly working his way through the solid oak door when he jumped up on it and scratched to let us know he was ready for supper.

Fortunately, most people's canines are a bit less inclined to treat their entire home as a chew toy, but you can still take inspiration from what I do to create the best outdoor living space for your non-human family members.

In general, an appropriate environment for maximum canine happiness includes natural vegetation, soft earth that supports excavation, brush that provides cover, varied elevations that allow animals to find shade or observe the world from high vantage points, and sufficient space that your dog can stretch its legs into a run before having to come up short to avoid running into a fence. The benefits of a habitat designed with your dog in mind will be evident once you make the adaptations.

Think Habitat, not Enclosure

When animals live in a biologically appropriate and naturally enriched habitat, you'll see a marked difference in their behavior. Happy animals are not actively looking for a means to get out. So, while my animals are always excited to go on a patrol, in nearly 40 years, I've never had one that tried to engineer an escape from our collective home. Meanwhile, just in my small town, people's domestic dogs escape all the time. Some of this is because people are lazy and are unwilling to invest in creating adequate security for their canine companions. But it's also because the environment they've provided is uninteresting and inadequate for an animal as intelligent and active as a youthful domestic dog.

"When Your Husky Gets Loose, the Neighbor Calls,
When Your Wolves Get Loose, the Newspaper Calls."

Nunarjuaq gets his feet wet. In addition to natural surfaces and vegetation, we provide a swimmable water source for our animals.

For my part, I've invested decades in understanding how to build the best and most appropriate habitats that withstand years of severe weather and incorporate our beautiful natural surroundings without looking like a compound, and increases the value of our home rather than detracting from it. I build habitats of several acres in scope and use ornamental iron fencing, ground wire, and, because where I live, we can get 700 inches of snow in some winters, electrified wire that allows me to increase the height of the fence as required. Granted, unless you've got a belligerent husky, you probably don't need to go anywhere near the extremes I do to make sure my habitats are secure. But then, when your husky gets loose, the neighbor calls. When your wolves get loose, the newspaper calls, and I don't want to be in the newspaper for something like that.

So, let's talk about an appropriate habitat for your canine companion. Undoubtedly, not everyone has the resources to provide the habitat I do for our animals, but then you probably aren't trying to keep wolves in your suburban neighborhood either, and if you are, you should consider relocating. A suburban environment isn't a good place for a wolf or high-content wolfdog. You may not have acreage available, but that's okay, especially if your domestic companion spends significant time accompanying you, both in the house and when you leave it. An extensive habitat is not nearly as important for a domestic dog as a wolf.

Building a Backyard Habitat

But even a residential backyard can be an appropriate habitat or an inappropriate prison, depending on what you do with it. A perfectly square, bowling-green lawn may look delightful for humans, but it may as well be a jail cell for a dog. If you want to do right by your canine companion, take inspiration from the habitats experts build. Leave some bare earth so your dog can dig holes. If your property doesn't allow for natural elevation, create it by building platforms. Ensure they have a space on top and space underneath to get out of the weather and the sun.

It's essential that your habitat is connected to your home and not separated from it. When your home and the place where your dog spends most of its time are separate, you're sending the message to your dog that she isn't part of your family. This separation is psychologically devastating for most canines since their human family means everything to them. If you have a fenced backyard, ensure your animal has direct access to some portion of your home. That doesn't mean they need free access to the interior, but if you can simply open a door to allow ingress or egress, you're sending the message that your dog is part of the family and not a prisoner kept on the outskirts of the human habitation.

The critical things to consider when designing your habitat are the aesthetics of what you've built so you don't upset your neighbors, the durability and security of your perimeter fence, the environment where you're building, and the nature of your animals. Large, powerful dogs tend to be the most difficult to contain, but there are miniature breeds that are **ferocious** diggers that come with their own set of challenges, none of which are insurmountable, so long as you're willing to expend a little bit of money and perhaps a bit more effort.

One more thing—keep the habitat clean. Nothing disgusts and disappoints me like visiting someone's property and seeing the place where their dogs spend much of their time defiled with piles of excrement. Your dog deserves better! Not only can excess feces attract insects and other parasites, but it's also a vector for disease, and inevitably your dog—or you—are going to step in it and bring it into your house. I always have a roll of poop bags in my pocket and typically pick up any poop the moment I notice it. I also walk the habitat a minimum of twice a day to check the fencelines and verify everything is secure. During this time I also monitor and pick up shredded toys, the remains of any stolen item, and whatever else I notice.

Wolfy Wisdom

So, what is the Wolfy Wisdom when it comes to rethinking backyard prisons and turning them into biologically appropriate habitats? Simple. Consider the environment from the perspective of your dog. Do they have places that are interesting to them, that allow them to exert their natural inclinations? Dogs like to dig. They like to hide. They like to run. They like to observe the world around them from different vantage points. They like to have the opportunity to enjoy sunbathing, and they appreciate being able to get out of the sun and the weather as their mood and needs see fit.

If you need inspiration, look no further than an AZA-accredited wildlife facility with captive wolves. Most of those facilities have live cameras into their habitats, and you can see what a well-designed, biologically appropriate habitat for any canine, no matter how robust, should look and feel like for the dog.

Sunny and Nepenthe look right at home in the wilds of their biologically appropriate habitat.

Natural habitats mean happy animals. Here, Aqutaq, Taqqiq, and Nunarjuaq sing the song of their people.

Iqniq exhibiting an appropriate territorial reaction as he notices coyotes on the other side of our habitat fence.

Part 3:

Behaviors, not Problems

In the first two parts of this book, I've devoted much of the text to methods to improve the world your dog shares with you and to help you understand how to leverage the underlying basis for much canine behavior to create a more dog-friendly environment. In part three, I continue to look at the basis for behaviors, but in these chapters, I examine behaviors often seen as problematic with a focus on understanding why your dog might do something and how you can understand and even reduce some of them.

He's not broken, he's reactive!

Chapter 15:

Your Reactive Dog Isn't Broken

The Most Common Challenge With Dogs

The most common and intractable issue people experience in dog training circles is broadly categorized as canine reactivity. Reactivity can be as simple as your dog excessively barking at any stimulus to very specific reactive behaviors, such as aggression towards a particular kind of dog or even a specific individual.

If your canine companion is exhibiting severe and potentially dangerous reactions to certain stimuli, it is crucial that you contact a qualified and accredited canine behavioral consultant[29] to help you manage the issue and

---

29   The top accreditations for canine behavioral consultants include:
Certified Applied Animal Behaviorist (CAAB) / Associate Certified Applied Animal Behaviorist (ACAAB)
Offered by the Animal Behavior Society (ABS), these certifications are for professionals with advanced degrees (Ph.D. or Master's) in animal behavior, along with practical experience.
Certified Professional Dog Trainer - Knowledge Assessed (CPDT-KA) / Certified Professional Dog Trainer - Knowledge and Skills Assessed (CPDT-KSA)
Provided by the Certification Council for Professional Dog Trainers (CCPDT), these certifications require passing a comprehensive exam and, for CPDT-KSA, a practical skills assessment.
Certified Dog Behavior Consultant (CDBC)
Issued by the International Association of Animal Behavior Consultants (IAABC), this certification is for those who have demonstrated extensive experience and knowledge in dog behavior consulting.
Associate Certified Dog Behavior Consultant (ACDBC)

reduce the risk to yourself or your family. However, it's important to note that reacting to their environment is critical to the behavior of canines. In fact, reactivity is one of the things that early humans leveraged as dogs morphed from wild animals into our most trusted non-human companions. For example, wolves don't bark, but dogs do. And for good reason. Your dog's alarming vocalizations that get you in hot water with your neighbors were originally a highly desirable attribute for humans long before security systems were invented; barking was a trait our ancestors wanted in their first non-human family members. In other words, your reactive dog is not broken, she's doing precisely what early humans wanted when dogs co-evolved with our early ancestors.

In the wild, wolves react to virtually everything in their environment. Sometimes, the reaction is as simple as ears pricking up or tuning in to a movement in the grass. Other times, they'll notice movement in the distance and alert to it, attracting the attention of their family members. What distinguishes the reactivity of wild animals from that of domestic dogs is the appropriateness and specificity of their reactions. The real challenge is not that your dog reacts, but that it overreacts to the point where the behavior seems unmanageable.

Also from the IAABC, this certification is for those who have some experience in dog behavior consulting but have not yet met all the requirements for the CDBC.
Diplomate of the American College of Veterinary Behaviorists (DACVB)
This is the highest level of certification for veterinary behaviorists, requiring a veterinary degree and extensive post-graduate training in animal behavior.
Fear Free Certified Professional
Provided by Fear Free Pets, this certification focuses on reducing fear, anxiety, and stress in pets during veterinary visits and other interactions.
Karen Pryor Academy Certified Training Partner (KPA-CTP)
Offered by the Karen Pryor Academy for Animal Training & Behavior, this certification emphasizes positive reinforcement training methods.
Victoria Stilwell Academy for Dog Training and Behavior - Certified Dog Trainer (VSA-CDT)
This certification is provided by the Victoria Stilwell Academy, known for its focus on positive, humane dog training methods.
National Association of Dog Obedience Instructors (NADOI) Certification
This certification is for professional dog trainers who meet NADOI's standards of experience and expertise.
Academy for Dog Trainers Certification
Offered by the Academy for Dog Trainers, this certification is known for its rigorous curriculum and focus on evidence-based training methods.

Aqutaq displays classic resource-guarding behavior with a fish head! For wolves, controlling a resource is life-or-death.

Sharpeners and Levelers

Decades of observing the behavior of social carnivores, like wolves, in the wild have yielded some eye-opening insights. One is the difference in the appropriate reactions of animals who are typically the decision-makers among social carnivores and those that follow along. Broadly categorized, these animals fall into two distinct groups: Sharpeners and Levelers.[30] The Sharpeners tend to be the ones making the decisions. Let me explain the difference so you understand why.

In response to some novel stimulus, the animals known as Levelers have an abrupt reaction that tends to attenuate as they observe the stimulus and then adjust their responses as required. In other words, their reactions spike and then level out. Typically, this is accompanied by heightened alertness, increased respiratory and heart rate, elevated blood pressure, and narrowed pupils. In other words, they get adrenalized first, and then, as the adrenaline spike attenuates, they calm a bit in response to the stimulus. From a leadership standpoint, the problem with this behavior is that it might provoke excessive and unnecessary reactivity amongst the other social group members, and the reactions may be wholly inappropriate. For example, there's no reason to have your adrenaline spike due to a butterfly.

On the other hand, Sharpeners exhibit very different physiological and intellectual responses when presented with the same stimuli. They pause. They ascertain the stimulus's nature and sharpen their reaction as appropriate. Sometimes, their ears prick, they look in the direction of the stimulus, they realize it's not important, and they go back to sleep. Other times, they identify unfamiliar wolves coming over a ridgeline. And, of course, they bring all their resources to bear and marshal the other members of their family group with an appropriate and most likely aggressive or defensive response. It makes sense that you want your generals to determine what's happening before deciding how to react. In other words, Levelers are ready, fire, aim, and Sharpeners are ready, aim, fire. It's a critical distinction.

Based on Kira Cassidy's research and her conflict matrix, which I mentioned a few chapters back, I contend that older wolves mature into Sharpeners, regardless of whether they were Sharpeners or Levelers, to begin with. All

30   Mech, L. David. "The Wolf: The Ecology and Behavior of an Endangered Species." University of Minnesota Press, 1981.
Bekoff, Marc, and Michael A. Allen. "The Evolution of Social Play: Interactions among Jaguars, Wolves, and Dolphins." In "Play, Playfulness, Creativity, and Innovation," Cambridge Scholars Publishing, 2017.

wolves and wild social carnivores likely start as levelers. However, as their experience and wisdom increase, their library of alarming stimuli becomes deeper and their catalog of appropriate responses broader.

The Vicious Cycle of Reactive Reactivity in Multi-Dog Household

As a result, hyper-reactive dogs tend to get stuck in the leveler phase. They don't learn how to sharpen to the correct environmental stimulus appropriately. Worse, their reactivity feeds on itself. And before long, any stimulus generates a reactive response, and the reactive response increases reactivity. You'll also see this happen in multi-canine households, where one reactive dog overstimulates all the other dogs. Before long, you've got canine mayhem as all the animals react, not just to the stimulus but to the reactions of the other dogs and even their human caretakers.

In many cases, reactivity can become self-reinforcing. For example, if your dog barks as people and dogs walk in front of your home, and the barking causes the person and their dog to move on more quickly, the reactive barking is rewarded with the desired result leading to more reactive barking in the future.

Compounding the problem for families with more than one canine, especially those with a variety of breeds in the same household, is the composition of the group and the different behavioral dynamics typical of any specific breed.

I've seen these issues crop up often. One example is in high-drive herding dogs, such as Border Collies, Queensland Heelers, or Australian Shepherds, all these breeds are known for their intense work ethic and need for mental and physical stimulation. These dogs are bred to herd livestock, and their instincts can present significant challenges in a family setting, especially one with young children.

Herding dogs may try to herd children, often nipping at their heels or chasing them as they would with livestock. This behavior can be frightening and potentially dangerous for small children who may not understand the dog's intentions.

These breeds typically require a high level of physical exercise and mental stimulation to prevent boredom and the development of destructive behaviors. Families that cannot provide adequate outlets for their energy may find themselves dealing with behavioral issues such as excessive barking, chewing, or digging.

Breeds like German Shepherds or Rottweilers are often chosen for their protective instincts and loyalty to their families. However, these same traits can become problematic in specific household environments, particularly if the family is not prepared to manage them.

These dogs are naturally protective and can be wary of strangers. In a busy household with many visitors, the dog may become overly protective, leading to aggressive behaviors towards guests.

Guard dogs require consistent training and socialization to ensure they can distinguish between real threats and normal social interactions. Without proper training, their natural protectiveness can escalate into unmanageable aggression.

Recently, I've noticed a lot of livestock guarding dogs in need of rescue. People often have significant challenges with livestock guarding dogs, especially if they adopted one without understanding the nature of the breed's typical behavior, and especially if they live in an environment that's not ideal for the breed, such as an urban or suburban location where the dog's natural inclinations may be off-putting or frightening to neighbors. It takes an especially committed family, like my brother Joseph's, to successfully integrate a livestock guarding dog into an urban environment.

Livestock guarding dogs are incredibly family-oriented. The entire basis for the breed is protecting the family and the family's livestock and alerting the family to any potential threat. In other words, their programming is to react to anything other than family, bark first to alert the family, then bite if necessary. It's virtually impossible to train those behaviors out of an animal selectively bred to have those behaviors in the first place.

However, if you have any breed of dog that tends toward high-intensity behaviors plus any other dog breed, your problem just gets exponentially worse. That's because the behavior of one dog will initiate that behavior in another dog. The last thing you want, for example, is the alertness of a livestock guarding dog and the protective, aggressive drive of a Malinois. You can see why that situation could portend disaster.

Ideally, people do some breed research before they decide to add a new non-human family member, and they make their selection based on understanding worst-case scenarios and what that looks like in conjunction with their lifestyle. Unfortunately, most people don't make their family acquisition decisions so judiciously, and you end up with canines set up to fail because the people didn't know what they were getting into.

If you find yourself in this situation, read on. While I don't propose training the behavior a dog was bred to exhibit out of the dog, I do have suggestions for ameliorating the intensity and helping you redirect those behaviors in more appropriate directions.

Why There Are Hundreds of "Big White Fluffy Dogs" on My Facebook Page

You only have to look at my Facebook page to see the thousands of Huskies, Malinois, Great Pyrenees, and other more primitive large breeds I share nearly daily because their families couldn't manage them.

Generally, all of the dogs I listed above are intelligent, high-drive dogs that have been selectively bred for generations to do specific jobs. Not only are these among the smartest and most energetic breeds, but they also tend to be among the stubbornest. If you have your heart set on a canine of this type, it's imperative that you understand that these dogs need a job, and if you don't give them one, they'll find one for themselves and you probably won't like it.

The recipe for success with any of the breeds I mentioned is a commitment to training, exercise, a consistent routine, and an understanding of the demands these dogs place on their two-legged stewards. If you need help, identify a professional with any of the certifications I've listed in previous footnotes.

Most of these folks wanted Ghost from Game of Thrones or the "big white fluffy dog" their daughter demanded. Instead, they got more than they bargained for. Virtually all of these owner surrenders could have been avoided with a little bit of research and maybe a different decision at the outset. But that bird has flown by the time a dog ends up on my Facebook page.

If you're reading this book and struggling with reactivity, my goal isn't to teach you how to train it away—that's a different book by another expert. My focus is on helping you understand the basis for the behavior and giving you some simple tools to help you accommodate, adjust, and adapt.

Sunny pauses to sharpen her attention to something ahead on the trail.

Alphas? No. Sharpeners? Yes!

Remember that I believe there is no alpha, but that does not mean there is no leader. A competent human handler should lead by example and set the tone for their family group in everything they do. Leadership is critical when dealing with reactivity, yet the human family group leader frequently worsens the problem because of their reaction to the reactivity, in effect, leveling when the response that a reactive dog needs is to see their human sharpening.

If you know, for example, that you have a dog-aggressive dog and that dog tends to exhibit high reactivity on a leash when other dogs are approaching, your inclination is to become stressed out, annoyed, and defensive the moment you see an oncoming dog. You're anticipating conflict. And even if you don't exhibit those behaviors outwardly, your internal state manifests itself in micro-movements and odors that your canine will immediately pick up on.

As an aside, while I'm dictating this, I'm out with a couple of my animals and observing sharpening behavior in Sunny, one of my yearling pups, as I speak.

As we were walking, some noise or odor caught her attention. She stops and pauses, and now Sunny is scanning the brush to determine what exactly she heard or smelled. And now, I can hear it too. A large animal, probably a bear, is in the brush about a hundred yards from us. But as opposed to a dog having an inappropriate reaction, Sunny is calmly assessing the situation and because she's calm, my seven-month-old malamute pup is also calm. She's illustrating right now, non-verbally, better than I ever could with a description, appropriately sharpening to a stimulus and therefore not begetting reactivity in another, less experienced, animal. If you could listen to the audio, you'd hear nothing because they're absolutely silent while they assess the stimulus. There's no barking. There's no growling. She's not jerking at the end of the long line. She's simply scanning the environment to determine the nature of the noise and how to respond to it appropriately.

And this is precisely what humans with reactive dogs need to do. Particularly in the example I provided where you have a dog-aggressive, reactive dog, and you're dealing with an approaching dog that's likely to elicit a reaction, rather than anticipating a problem, it's better to be the calm and assured leader who makes a decision and takes action on it appropriately. In this case, I recommend calmly and casually changing your route. Don't engage with the other person or the dog and don't telegraph your concern to the dog that's with you. By not stimulating the reactive response, the dog doesn't get the adrenaline rush that begets the reactive behavior and creates a vicious cycle.

For me, this issue is particularly apropos. As I've mentioned many times, wolves and wolfdogs tend to be very territorial and highly aggressive towards canines that aren't part of their family group. The biggest challenge I experience when out with my animals is the individual who has an off-leash dog that isn't listening and doesn't respond to recall commands. If you shout out, "he's friendly," as your uncontrolled dog approaches someone else, what you're really saying is, "I have no control of my dog and whatever happens next is your problem." In other words, you're abdicating 100% of your responsibility for the animal in your care and putting all that burden and the risk on anybody else with whom that dog might interact.

For me, I'm not the least bit concerned that the dog isn't friendly. I'm concerned that if the dog gets too close, it might not survive the encounter. My animal's reaction is appropriate for what they are, and there's no way I'm going to train those behaviors out of my dogs. But what I try to do is anticipate those interactions and avoid them altogether. As I move away, I often calmly tell my animals, "We don't care."

One of the big problems I frequently see in people dealing with reactive dogs is the failure to anticipate the triggers and take appropriate action before the reactivity starts. A lot of this comes down to being in tune with your animal and the environment. So much of the time, people are with their dog, but they're not truly **with** their dog. If you're on your phone, checking your social media, conversing with a friend, or otherwise disengaged from the moment, you probably aren't going to identify, anticipate, and avoid situations that trigger reactivity.

Additionally, your response to the reactivity has the potential to reduce or aggravate the behavior. Rehearsal of behavior IS reinforcing, so if you have an overreactive dog, you should endeavor to manage these situations to the best of your ability to prevent rehearsal. Being in tune with your animal and the environment can go a long way toward reducing and even eliminating many reactive behaviors.

So what's the Wolfy Wisdom? First, understand that reactivity is normal and natural. It isn't a sign that something is wrong with your dog. It's your dog telling you that things in their environment cause them concern. Accepting that a certain amount of reactivity is normal and natural will help you feel better about the situation.

But digging deeper, understand that reactive behavior can also be self-affirming, creating a reaction to the reaction. It's this vicious cycle that we should strive to avoid, and the best way to do that is by identifying the triggers and taking action to avoid them. Granted, this is sometimes easier said than done, especially if you have multiple animals in your household, but the best thing you can do in response to reactive behavior is discipline yourself, not your dog.

If your dog's reactivity makes you react negatively, you can become an additional trigger. Wolves look to their leaders to determine how to respond in their environment, and you need to take on this calm, assured leadership role with your animals. Tune in to the environment and your dogs. Be present. Anticipate likely triggers. Identify situations that may provoke reactions and calmly move to avoid them before your dogs begin to react. Be the Sharpener in your family group.

Aqutaq says, "Make my day," as she resource-guards Sunny and Moonie in their "pup-tagon," canines can guard almost anything from locations to food to remote controls, or even, as in this case, 3-week-old pups.

Chapter 16:

Resource Guarding: Life or Death in the Wild

According to the American Veterinary Medical Association (AVMA), approximately 4.5 million dog bites occur in the United States each year. One of the most common reasons dogs bite their human family members is resource-guarding behavior. This statistic shouldn't be a surprise. Nothing is as hardwired into canine psychology as the drive to procure and consume sustenance.

For Wolf Puppies, Competition Starts at Birth

Think about it from an evolutionary perspective: Even tiny wolf puppies are competing for the most productive nipples. That competition intensifies as they solicit the mature wolves to regurgitate food and again when they are collectively feeding off a carcass. Once an animal has a desirable morsel, maintaining control of their meal is truly life or death. In the wild, you're dead if another animal can bully you and steal your lunch.

Frankly, I'm surprised there aren't more resource-guarding-related bite incidents. It shows you how good-natured our domestic canines are. Our dogs routinely allow human hands to take hold of what they're eating and even remove it from their mouths. However, not all dogs are so tolerant, and many end up dead or surrendered due to their natural inclination to protect what is theirs.

Hands Near Bowls Should Come Bearing Gifts

From my perspective, once a dog has full possession of something, particularly something you gave them like a bowl full of food, it's the height of poor judgment and bad canine stewardship to attempt to repossess what they now believe is theirs. When working with wolves, I accept that once they have something, I'm not getting it back, and I don't expect to. Although there are things I do to make resource guarding a bit less of an issue. One of the first things is to bring something better if I'm going to be near an animal that's eating. Human hands near food or a bowl should be offering gifts, not representing a threat.

Even so, it's not uncommon for our animals to give us a face full of teeth when I get anywhere near them while they're enjoying something tasty. One way I combat this is by hand-feeding all of our animals from their first days with our family. Often, this starts with the baby bottle I use when nursing tiny pups, but I continue this practice so that almost every calorie they consume for months, and sometimes even years, comes directly from my hands. Currently, I'm working with a puppy we rescued from the unlawful wildlife trade. Even though he's just a few months old, he is the most voracious and intense eater I've encountered in my 40 years working with the species. He's so aggressive about food that even though I've been hand-feeding him for the last three months, I still wear gloves to make sure I don't accidentally get nipped as I hand him each piece. I expect to hand-feed this animal for several more years, if not indefinitely. How long you hand feed depends on you and your dog. The more intense your canine is, the longer I suggest you hand-feed it, especially if your pup tends to be aggressive around food, toys, or even people.

I enjoy hand-feeding my animals, and because wolves and high-content wolfdogs tend to have such strong resource-guarding inclinations, I maintain this practice for years. Even when I stop regularly hand-feeding a particular animal, I'll still do a hand-feeding session once in a while to maintain that positive association between my hands and mealtime.

Train Your Child to Respect Your Dog

By ensuring that my hands are always associated with something positive, you reduce the likelihood that your dog will bite those hands at some point. Although I'm quite confident that if I attempt to repossess something Nunarjuaq is eating, he'll teach me a lesson and give me a toothy spanking. But I know better, and you should know better too. This fact is especially true in households with children. More than once, I've seen people punish their animal for growling at a child when the child was near the eating dog's bowl. This act is a mistake. Not only are you conditioning the wrong behavior, but you're teaching your child to be abusive to a dog for doing what it should be doing, which is protecting the thing it's eating. Better to teach your child to leave the dog to eat unmolested.

Furthermore, when people punish their dog for growling, you can staunch their ability to growl, eliminating a warning system that can make a dog more prone to agressing without warning.

The more you threaten an animal that has possession of something, particularly food, the more likely that animal is to become defensively aggressive as a result. And aggressive defense is biting defense. In other words, train your children, not the dog.

The Breed Most Likely to Bite

From "The Genius of Dogs" by Brian Hare and Vanessa Woods *"While we are not sure about breed differences when it comes to aggression, what science can tell us is that 70% of bites happen to children under the age of 10. More than 60% of the children bitten are boys and 87% are white. Children are most frequently bitten 61% of the time when they come in contact with the dog's food or possessions. The children will usually be injured in the head and neck area, 55% to the cheek and lips, with the average length of the wound being three inches. Most of the breeds involved are large dogs and male dogs are more likely to bite than female dogs. Two-thirds of the dogs who bite children have never before bitten a child and between 25 and 33% of the dogs who bit were family pets.*

In conclusion, the "breed" most likely to be involved in a severe dog-related injury is a child, usually a white male under age 10, with a large male dog living in the family home."

So what's the Wolfy Wisdom? Understand that resource guarding is natural and is not an aberrant behavior. Accept that some dogs, particularly more primitive dogs, are likely to be more intense, especially if they're eating something they genuinely enjoy. Resource guarding will be more likely with more desirable foods or if you're attempting to manage an overweight animal's diet with some caloric restriction. The same holds true for dogs who were calorie-starved at some point in their lives or had an ultra-competitive start where the ability to get and maintain control of food was a matter of life or death. Just like humans, the hungrier a dog is, the more likely it is to protect its food.

When I was a professional athlete, I had a teammate with 14 brothers and sisters. He once told me that food was always in short supply while he was growing up, and you could see this manifested in how he ate as an adult. He would cradle one arm around his entire bowl and keep his face close to his plate. More than once, when people encroached on him while he was eating, he inadvertently made a **guttural** sound that was almost a growl. If this behavior crops up in humans, imagine how much more intense it can be in the more primitive mind of a canine.

My advice is first to hand-feed your dogs, especially those that seem inclined to be more aggressive about resources. If you have multiple dogs, feed them separately so they don't compete with one another and create reciprocal resource guarding. The more dogs you have, the more important this becomes. When approaching a bowl that still has food, come in with something better. Your dogs are going to be much more inclined to see a hand favorably if the hand comes bearing gifts. And if your dog is exhibiting potentially dangerous resource-guarding behavior, start hand-feeding the dog every single thing.

One important thing to note about hand feeding is to avoid frustrating your dog with the pace of the feeding. Your goal here is not to require the dog to perform a behavior, but simply to understand that good things come from your hands. When I'm feeding a voracious animal, for example, like my most recent family member, Nunarjuaq, I found that my usual practice of holding on to a frozen log and allowing him to take bites of it was problematic. Nuni couldn't consume the food fast enough for his liking and he was interpreting my efforts to keep a hold of the log as trying to take it away. Once I realized this, thanks to a tip from fellow professional wolf handler Megan Glosson of Busch Gardens, who made her astute suggestion after I showed her a video of hand-feeding Nuni, I began cutting the log into bite-size chunks and feeding them to him one at a time. This small change made a world of difference in how he approached his meals and made the process much less stressful for him and easier for me.

Finally, educate your children that dogs are not playthings and mealtime is serious business. By encouraging them to be good canine stewards who respect your dogs, you dramatically reduce the risk of a resource-guarding-related bite incident. By allowing your dog to eat in peace with no stress or pressure from any human, their level of resource aggression will remain low or become reduced, if it exists at all.

Again, keep in mind that the drive to guard resources, including toys and even favorite people, not just food, is completely normal and natural, and dogs that don't resource guard are unusual canine citizens. Don't expect it, and you won't be surprised when the behavior crops up. Now, you'll know what to do to manage it more effectively if, or when, it does.

About to become a statistic! Aqutaq snaps when my hand comes too close to her bone.

Wild Box Kill Site! Nepenthe and Nunarjuaq discuss the disposition of the remains of a wild box after completing the carcass dissection.

Chapter 17

Good Gets and Wild Boxes. Rethinking Enrichment

In the United States, the pet food and treat market, which includes dog treats, was valued at around USD 36.1 billion in 2023 and is expected to grow at a CAGR of 8% through 2032. The size and scope of this market speak to our desire to augment our canine family members' lives with treats, toys, and all manner of purchased goodies.

Although there are some good things to be found among the vast array of commercial pet products, there are myriad ways to enrich the lives of your furry people more economically and better yet, without the risk inherent in many products that have the potential to sicken or injure your pet. This is unfortunate, especially when you discover that simple things, like soft earth, a pumpkin, or the Amazon box you just opened will delight your pet at nearly no cost, and without a trip to the pet store.

By providing regular enrichment for your non-human family members, you'll not only entertain yourself and your dogs, but you'll also gain the not-insignificant benefit of better canine behavior. Intellectually engaged, properly enriched dogs are calmer, less destructive, and even tend to be better about destroying what you want them to destroy, rather than something you'd prefer they leave intact.

In this chapter, I'll tell you some of our favorite tricks of the trade and even regale you with the day I came home to a scene that looked like Aqutaq had killed a robot.

Wild Boxes

In front of our mailbox and posted conspicuously in two additional locations along my drive are notices to delivery personnel that read, "Attention delivery drivers, please place boxes in the indicated bin to the left of the drive. Do not place near fence or gate; dogs will destroy."

You see, our animals love delivery drivers. They believe they come bearing gifts. That's because there's nothing so enticing to our animals as what I call wild boxes. A wild box is any package that comes from outside the property without us handling it first. A wild box smells different, and inside, there are often surprises.

Once, a delivery driver placed a wild box right in front of our gate containing an all-in-one printer, fax, and copier unit. Unfortunately for us, he put it there while I was away from the property. By the time I returned home, Aqutaq had pulled the box and the machine through the fence, piece by piece. When I arrived, it looked like she had killed a mechanical animal. No piece surviving was larger than a silver dollar.

It's hard to comprehend a wolf's destructive capability unless you've seen it firsthand. I'm talking about every bit of cardboard, styrofoam, circuit boards, plastic casing, and every other piece of the unit. I took a photograph of the damage and requested Amazon refund the purchase with the option I selected as delivered damaged. I was incredulous when Amazon gave me a refund.

You probably don't run the risk of your animals doing something similar, but you can take inspiration from the experience and leverage new forms of enrichment that your animals will love every bit as much as an expensive, artificial, manufactured dog toy.

Good Gets

Unfortunately, this is not the extent of the mischief I've experienced in our decades living inside our wolf habitat. Our animals frequently dart into the house when we've been lax about closing a door, and when they do, a "good get" frequently occurs.

A good get is when one of the animals grabs something of ours and makes it out the door and into the habitat before I can head them off and attempt to broker a trade. And once something is out the door, the odds of recovering the item in recognizable condition are long indeed.

It's not the least bit unusual for me to be patrolling our fenceline (a twice-daily activity) only to discover the remains of a shoe, an area rug, a remote control, or something else that got by me when a wolf executed a successful heist. I accept these stolen items as the cost of how I live, and over the years, I've realized that our animals are quicker than I am and, just like their wild conspecifics, being opportunistic hunters, they're primed and willing to exploit every available opportunity.

Our local cell phone repair shop has profited considerably from this problem. Aqutaq, our matriarch and the animal I lovingly call Princess BitchyPants because she's so spicy, has a particular affinity for my cell phones. I used to call her Two-Phone-Qu a decade ago (from her name pronounced Ah-koo-tahk), but that was at least seven cell phone screens ago. So successful is she at stealing my mobile devices that when I ring up Alpine Computers, the owner, Chris, answers the phone with, "Which device needs a new screen courtesy of your wolf?" I wish I could say I've learned to avoid this problem, but that would give me too much credit and wolves too little.

In the wild, wolves routinely provide pups with novel items for them to enjoy. Last year, using some of its trail cameras, the Yellowstone Wolf Project documented a two-year-old wolf laboriously carrying an entire elk's head miles back to the rendezvous site where the puppies were being cared for.

Wild Wolves Love Toys, Too

There was no good reason for the wolf to have expended so much energy carrying something so heavy back to the RZ, the abbreviation scientists use to indicate the rendezvous zone where pups reside once they leave a den. When the animal returned to the pups, they spent days enjoying, tussling over, and playing with this completely novel gift from an uncle.

You can provide interesting enrichment for your animals the same way we and other wolf caretaking professionals do. Recycling the myriad delivery boxes you receive each week is one of the easiest and most economical ways to enrich the lives of your canine kids. Get creative! You can put treats in the box, renew the remains of previously discarded toys, add essential oil to the surface to add a novel olfactory component, and even wrap the box with tape to increase the challenge. The only downside is that you might discover your home has the added charm of small bits of cardboard confetti. But the small inconvenience of picking up the pieces pales compared to the enjoyment you'll get from seeing how much fun your dog can have with a box.

My brother has his own twist on wild boxes for his cattle dogs. He balls up or shreds newspaper, and conceals small bite-sized treats throughout. His pups will dive in and excavate until they've consumed every morsel.

These alternative enrichment techniques keep our animals occupied without the cost of plastic, nylon, and polyester toys, especially when the wolves will reduce those same toys to an acre of polyester fluff in less than an hour.

Biologically Appropriate Enrichment

But that's not the extent of our enrichment library. Anything that's safe to consume can go into the habitat. I take seasonal inspiration by, for example, filling pumpkins with treats and freezing them, filling turkey carcasses with treats and freezing those. In hotter months, we do things like sardine popsicles, frozen mousicles, and other assorted yummies that are completely novel to our furry family members.

For those of you with large primitive dogs, whole rabbits make excellent enrichment, and they're frequently available at a fraction of the cost of manufactured dog toys. The added benefit is that the consumption of rabbits is excellent for your animals. In fact, tearing through hair and hide is the natural equivalent of a toothbrush for wild canines, which is one of the reasons why their teeth tend to be in better shape than the teeth of our domestic dogs.

While we'll cover feeding in a subsequent chapter, I can wholly endorse the idea of identifying interesting and fully consumable body parts as enrichment for the critters. These include duck and chicken feet, rabbit legs, whole rabbits, and the raw sections of chicken and other fowl, excluding turkeys unless you have big dogs. Contrary to the myth, it's not raw bones that pose a risk to dogs, including raw chicken bones, but rather cooked bones that become indigestible and therefore represent a hazard because they've been cooked.

Antler Chews? No Bueno!

Lately, dozens of companies are advertising deer antlers as the ultimate dog chew on websites like Facebook. Their advertising is compelling, and the idea behind purchasing an all-natural, exotic chew is tempting, but don't do it. Nothing is responsible for more broken canine teeth than deer antler chews. Ask your vet if you don't believe me. Wolves don't chew deer antlers, and dogs shouldn't either. [31]

Deer antlers are an incredibly hard material, keratin, much harder than bone. It has no nutritional value once the velvet is off it, and it's been dried like those sold commercially. Not only are they exceptionally expensive, but they can cost you thousands of dollars in veterinary bills when you try to rebuild shattered teeth because your dog was an aggressive chewer with an inappropriate treat.

Catnip for Wolves

One other thing we've discovered is that our animals especially love lemongrass. I grow it in large pots and occasionally put a pot out for the animals. They have a field day chewing the grass down to nubs, then rolling in the stems and stalks. Not only does it make your animal smell delicious and freshen its breath, but it has additional nutritional benefits.

31   https://www.whole-dog-journal.com/health/are-antlers-safe-for-dogs/

Wild Salad Bars

I routinely take my animals to areas where fresh grasses grow. In fact, while I'm dictating this, I'm watching Sunny and Nuni snack on something I call a salad bar, which is a permanent seep where the ground stays wet all year, allowing fresh grass to grow all the way until winter. Our animals love consuming these grasses. They act as an intestinal scour, a refreshing dietary novelty, and indeed they have other benefits we have yet to identify since canines seem to thrive when they have access to wild grasses.

Dryer Balls?

When heelers get a mouthful of wool while working with sheep, their trainers call it dental floss. Not only is this funny, but it's also true. Hair and hide do an admirable job of helping keep canine dentition clean and healthy. Wolves don't get dental cleanings, yet having teeth remain healthy is life or death for wild carnivores, so how does that happen? Nature has elegant solutions to many problems, and wolves brush their teeth by tearing through hair and hide and gnawing on bones.

Whenever we get the chance to collect a reasonably fresh roadkill, we jump at the chance. Having a neighbor call us to alert us to a downed deer gets us out the door in seconds to collect the valuable remains that serve as food and superb enrichment.

But not everyone is as keen as I am to clean and section a big dead animal.

Luckily, we've discovered that 100% wool organic dryer balls are an interesting substitute. For an added canine kick, you can add a canine-safe essential oil like catnip—yes, dogs appreciate catnip, too![32,33]

---

32   https://a.co/d/bgvjgpa
33   https://a.co/d/3cf1kO6

My brother's dog, Smidge post her evening dental hygiene routine. She's a fan of dryer balls, too!

Wolfy Wisdom

So what's the Wolfy Wisdom? If your animals love stuffies, indulge them occasionally, but don't rely on store-bought treats exclusively. Be more creative in your application of things you find around your house. Vary what you provide seasonally as appropriate and have fun with the exercise. Animals given novel enrichment are happy because their world is broadened as a result. There's nothing quite so delightful for us as watching a wolf roll a pumpkin up and down a hill, waiting for it to break apart and spill the contents. Your dogs will love them too, I promise.

Wolf dental floss. Aqutaq enjoys her big birthday prize, an entire deer carcass. Not only does breaking down a carcass provide critical nutrition and dental benefits, but the intellectual challenge of taking the animal apart combined with the vigilance associated with guarding the kill is one of the best enrichment options we can provide.

Chapter 18:

Feed Your Dog Like a Wolf

This chapter will likely be the most controversial one in my book. Nothing elicits opinions like the topic of how to feed your dog. Wolves don't eat kibble, and dogs shouldn't either. Many people are unaware that the commercial dog food market is a super profitable means of disposing of waste from human food production, despite the pretty pictures their marketing departments paint.

Pet Food: Biologically Hazardous Waste by Another Name

Decades ago, I wrote a now-out-of-print book called "The Dirty Truth of Commercial Pet Food," nothing has changed in the last 25 years. If you care to do the digging, you'll discover that virtually every single commercial pet food brand, no matter how expensive its product, is a subsidiary of a much larger conglomerate that makes food for people. This fact should come as no surprise since anything unsuitable for human consumption that's a foodstuff must be disposed of at a cost—unless, of course, you can turn that something into an incredibly profitable second revenue stream in the form of animal food.

For example, when livestock arrives at a slaughterhouse in unsalable condition, which means it's dead on arrival, obviously diseased, or dying before handling, those animals must be disposed of, and they're not used for the pink slime we call our hamburgers. Instead, 3D meat ends up slotted for animal food production. Hardly the pretty pictures that dog food companies want you to believe their products consist of. Not only is this awful meat at the outset but because of its disgusting and potentially toxic nature, it's cooked and combined with non-nutritive fillers like corn or pea protein or other biologically inappropriate foodstuffs that contribute to the bulk of the product.

Needless to say, we feed our animals a non-commercial raw diet and we encourage every canine caretaker to do the same. While it may seem daunting to go from buying a bag of dog food at Costco to procuring and preparing nutritious canine cuisine, I assure you it's easier than you think and the benefits to your dog will be significant. So, this begs the question—what do wolves, and by extension dogs, eat?

While wolves are not obligate carnivores, they're close. By weight, more than 90% of a wolf's diet consists of animal products, with a tiny percentage coming from ripe fruits and the intestinal contents of the animals wolves prey upon. Close association with humans has somewhat altered canine digestion, and some breeds of dogs now have enough of the enzyme amylase to break down starches, but wolves are incapable of digesting carbohydrates, and wolves fed kibble fare poorly.

So what does this have to do with how to feed your dogs? When you look at the label on any commercial pet food, you'll see a section called "Guaranteed Nutritional Analysis."

Here's an example of one from a well-known (and expensive) brand of premium dog food:

Guaranteed Analysis:

- Crude Protein (min) 23.0%
- Crude Fat (min) 13.0%
- Crude Fiber (max) 5.0%
- Moisture (max) 10.0%
- Calcium (min) 0.8%
- Phosphorus (min) 0.7%
- Vitamin E (min) 140 IU/kg

* Omega-6 Fatty Acids (min) 1.75%

Breaking Down the Guaranteed Analysis:

1. **Crude Protein (min) 23.0%:**
   * This figure indicates that the food contains at least 23% protein. Protein is essential for building and maintaining muscle mass and supporting the dog's overall growth and development.

2. **Crude Fat (min) 13.0%:**
   * This number signifies that the food contains at least 13% fat. Fat is a concentrated energy source and provides essential fatty acids, vital for healthy skin and coat.

3. **Crude Fiber (max) 5.0%:**
   * This percentage shows that the food contains no more than 5% fiber. Fiber aids in digestion and helps maintain healthy bowel movements.

4. **Moisture (max) 10.0%:**
   * This stat indicates that the food contains no more than 10% moisture. Moisture content is important to know because it affects the concentration of nutrients in the food.

5. **Calcium (min) 0.8%:**
   * This amount specifies that the food contains at least 0.8% calcium. Calcium is crucial for strong bones and teeth.

6. **Phosphorus (min) 0.7%:**
   * This figure shows that the food contains at least 0.7% phosphorus. Phosphorus works with calcium to maintain bone health and supports energy production.

7. **Vitamin E (min) 140 IU/kg:**
   * This information indicates that the food contains at least 140 International Units of Vitamin E per kilogram. Vitamin E is an antioxidant that helps protect cells from damage and supports immune function.

8. **Omega-6 Fatty Acids (min) 1.75%:**
   * This detail signifies that the food contains at least 1.75% omega-6 fatty acids, which are essential for maintaining healthy skin and a shiny coat.

If you're a keen student of human food nutrition labels, you'll probably notice a gaping hole here: carbohydrates. When you add up all of the items listed, you can come up with a rough estimate of the carbohydrate content of the food. I get 42%!

Wolves fed a diet of 42% carbohydrate would begin to exhibit health issues, as do many dog breeds. In spite of what the manufacturers of these products might claim, a diet this high in carbohydrates is far from ideal for animals descended from nearly obligate carnivores.

Wild Diets Are Healthier

In a fascinating study performed several years ago at the Wolf Conservation Center in New York,[34] scientists examined the gut biome of wolves fed three distinct diets. One group was fed whole carcasses, the natural food source for wolves in the wild. A second was fed commercially prepared raw diets intended to provide wolves with an analogous, though not identical, macronutrient breakdown. Finally, a group of wolves got kibble. They found something remarkable when they examined the microbiome of the wolves' intestines by looking at their feces. The wolves fed the whole carcass had both the most complex and the healthiest gut biome. In second place were the wolves fed a biologically appropriate, though commercial, diet. Finally, with a legitimately unhealthy gut microbiome, were the wolves fed a high-grade kibble product. These animals had fungal overgrowths, including candida and yeast, and their microbiome was far simpler than the other two groups.

So why is a more complex gut biome better? Good question. Having varied microbiota in the gut appears to provide significant immunological benefits that help ward off the health problems observed in the kibble-fed wolves. Studies have found that not only wolves but also dogs and cats with a more complex gut biome have better nutrient absorption, lower rates of infectious, particularly intestinal diseases, and overall better health.[35]

The Poop Tells the Tale

I was unsurprised by these findings. I've been feeding wolves and wolfdogs for almost 40 years, and I can tell you by how their feces look whether my animals are fed appropriately or not. I can also tell by looking at dog poop what other pet owners are feeding their dogs. Canines fed a raw diet have stools that resemble those of their wild counterparts, whereas canines

---

34   https://pmc.ncbi.nlm.nih.gov/articles/PMC7693430/
35   https://academic.oup.com/af/article/14/3/46/7696634

fed commercial kibble have poop that looks like giant sausage loaves. The poops are vastly enlarged compared to normal, healthy canine feces. My brother, who has worked with some of the world's more prominent dog food brands, told me that during one photo shoot, one of their people confided in us that they engineer the food to produce stools like this—consumers think the food is "working better" if when it comes out it's voluminous and round. But this perception isn't a good one. Small, dense, well-formed, and tapered feces indicate a proper diet fed in the appropriate amount for your animal.

A healthy canine poop is well-formed, dense, uniform, and looks like wild animal poop.

Further, if you examine the poop of kibble-fed dogs, you'll note that it has a granular appearance. What you're seeing are the undigested grains that are passing through the animal intact. Kibble also contains substantial amounts of preservatives, fillers, and synthetic vitamins because the nutritional value of the underlying proteins has been badly compromised and denatured by heating, frying, and cooking. Typically, these products are also rancid in the bag, and that's not hard to discern. Just open a bag of dog food and take a whiff.[36,37,38]

Veterinarians Fear Raw Diets, but You Don't Need to

Many veterinarians advocate commercial diets, either because they were indoctrinated into that way of thinking at their veterinary college, or because they are concerned that the average pet owner cannot successfully prepare a raw diet for their pet. It bears mentioning that Hills/Science Diet and other commercial pet food companies are significant benefactors of leading veterinary schools.

These concerns are largely unfounded, and great tutorials on making raw food for your dog are available on YouTube. There are countless books on raw feeding, with my favorite being "Give Your Dog a Bone" by Dr. Ian Billinghurst, a colleague of mine. I routinely produce YouTube videos to show people how to make raw dog food and how we prepare diets for our animals.

My wife and I prepare over 400 pounds of wolf food every month. As a result of our long experience with raw diets, our animals live longer, healthier lives than almost any other dogs I'm aware of. My giant malamute, Bixby, recently passed away at nearly 14—five to six years longer than average for giant breed malamutes and two years longer than any malamute our veterinarian had previously treated. He was healthy until the last two weeks of his life when suddenly age caught up with him, and he passed at home in our kitchen, the place he loved the most. I attribute his longevity and health to the raw diet we prepare based on the macronutrient content of wild elk.

36   https://academic.oup.com/tas/article/5/3/txab071/6287114?login=false
37   https://www.whole-dog-journal.com/health/digestion/carbohydrates-and-your-dogs-digestive-system/
38   https://blog.ultimatedog.com/grain-free-dog-food-good-or-bad/

My gauge for the biological appropriateness of the diet I feed my animals consists of annual blood work and urine tests that we increase to twice yearly once an animal reaches seven years of age, but more importantly, examining their feces on a daily basis. The poop tells you everything you need to know, and if the poop looks like a wild animal's poop, the diet is appropriate. If it doesn't, something needs to be tweaked.

How I Make Wolf Food

We rely principally on commercially available organic grass-fed beef to give people a basic idea of our typical preparation. Yes, it's expensive to feed wolves. Depending on the size and age of our animal, our guideline is roughly two pounds of protein and fat per day, with a ratio of 85% lean to 15% fat. The food we make contains virtually no carbohydrates, with the exception of organic kale.[39]

Our goal with our food is to duplicate as closely as possible what our animals would be eating in the wild. As I mentioned, the limited amount of vegetal matter that wild carnivores eat tends to be from their prey's partially digested intestinal contents.

Because wild canids lack amylase or cellulase, the enzymes necessary to break down plant cell walls and starches, we do the breaking down for them in a manner similar to the digestive process of their prey species.

Wild elk chew their food, and the acids in their stomach further break it down before passing it to the small intestine, where wolves consume it. To duplicate this process, we flash freeze the kale in a minus 20-degree freezer, then pulverize it by hand before mixing it with camelina oil, which acts as an acid to further break it down. Kale is mixed in a ratio of three and a half pounds of kale to each 25 pounds of protein.

In addition to the protein, camelina oil, and kale, we add a calcium and phosphorus mix, collagen, and pre and probiotic powder. Finally, to ensure our animals get all the essential fatty acids and other micronutrients they need, we mix in a commercial product called Platinum Performance CJ Plus.

---

39   https://youtube.com/live/G6k35dO1Vlo?feature=share (This is a full two-hour livestream of Thanya and me preparing 200 pounds of food for our canine family members.)

So successful is our diet that a number of the top facilities around the world now use ours as a model for their wild carnivore feeding programs. To prepare our food, we first slice all the meat and run it through a commercial beef slicer. Then we put it in 50-pound batches, add in the kale, the oil, and the powdered ingredients, and mix it by hand. Then we portion it into 2.3-pound servings, drop it into compostable plastic bags, and roll each bag like a burrito. Finally, we place that in the deep freeze until it's frozen solid. This process simplifies feeding dramatically for our animals. We take out six logs every evening, let them rest for about 20 to 30 minutes so they're not rock hard, and we hand each animal their own portion. For puppies, like my current rescue Nunaruaq, we hand-feed the animal by slicing the log into smaller pieces and parceling them out bit by bit.

A deeper dive into raw feeding is beyond the scope of this book, but I am available for raw feeding diet development consultations if you're interested in developing a custom program for your dog. So what's the Wolfy Wisdom here? Feed your dog like its wolf ancestors. Do not rely on commercially prepared products and look at their poop to determine if you're feeding your dog in a way that is optimal for their health and longevity.

A bonus tip: If you're struggling to prepare a raw diet, one alternative is to consider one of a very few brands of commercially prepared raw food or freeze-dried or air-dried food products. We typically have Real Meat Venison and Turkey Formula or ZiwiPeak Venison Formula in our go bags. These are super convenient and generally well tolerated; however, they are costly. If we were to feed those products to all our animals every day, our food cost would be over $150 a day. Needless to say, it's more economical to buy 400 pounds of meat a month than it is to buy the equivalent in a commercially prepared product with a profit margin built in. But if you have a smaller dog, a tight schedule, or a squeamish stomach, it is a viable alternative that should yield good results and healthy, normal-looking stools for almost all breeds of dogs.

Bonus tip number two: if you have access to fresh natural grass such as those that grow along streams, or in wild areas that are natural, indulge your pup's inclination to sample these "wild salad bars." Unlike commercial lawns that may be treated with herbicides and other chemicals, these natural, wild grasses are a healthful adjunct to your dog's diet, acting as an intestinal scour, freshening their breath, helping to remove plaque and tartar from their teeth, and providing them with a dietary diversion during a walk.

Wolf mom in her wolf apron making wolf food. You can't get much wolfier than that!

Wolf Birthdays are serious business at our house. Here's the bountiful buffet we've prepared in celebration of Iqniq's fifth journey around the sun. In case you're wondering, this was before Nunarjuaq joined our family.

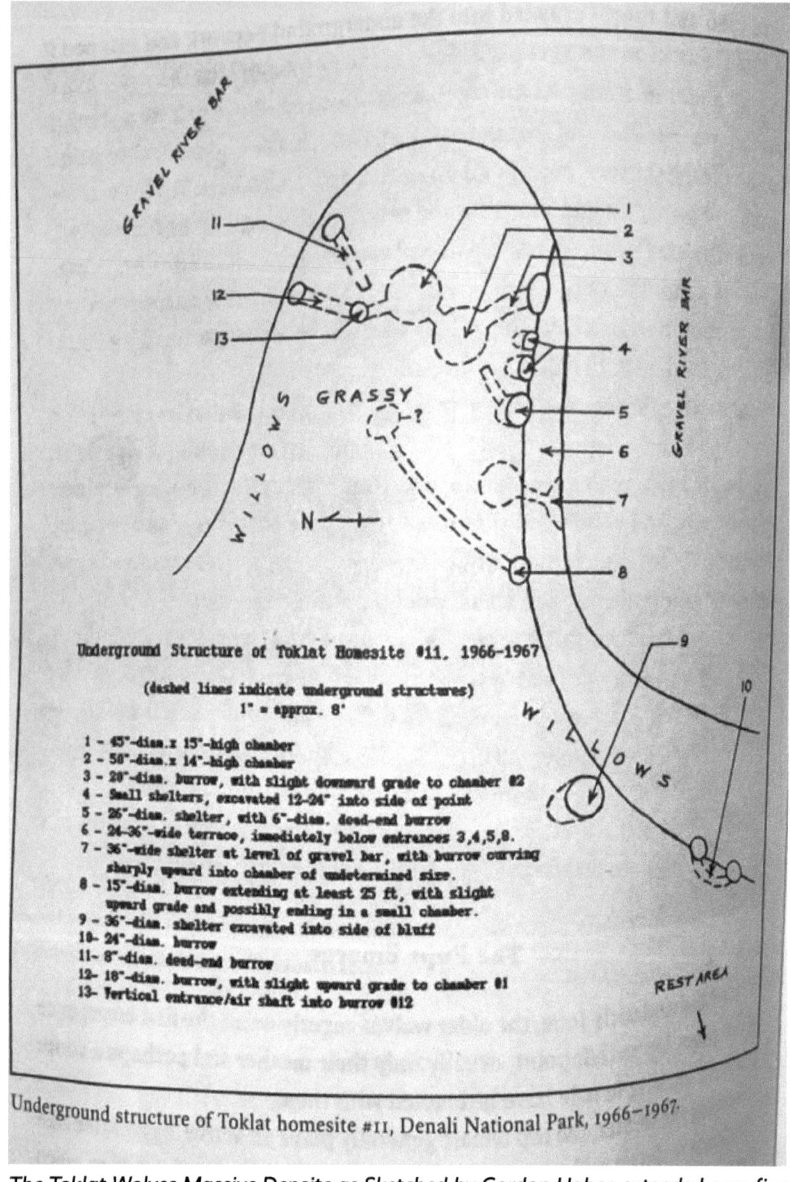

Underground structure of Toklat homesite #11, Denali National Park, 1966–1967.

The Toklat Wolves Massive Densite as Sketched by Gordon Haber, extended over five kilometers and had been inhabited, and improved upon, by hundreds of generations of wolves. To Haber, and to me, this is documentary evidence of culture in wolves.

Chapter 19

Establishing a Canine Culture

Wolf Dynasties - Ancient Canine Culture

In 2013, while observing wolves in Yellowstone National Park, I struck up a conversation with wolf biologist Rick McIntyre, arguably the man who has spent more time observing Yellowstone's wolves than anyone else alive. He mentioned his observation, echoed by another legendary wolf biologist, Gordon Haber, that wolf family groups establish a culture. This culture persists as long as the family group remains intact over generations.

Haber and McIntyre observed that the cultural distinctions of the groups they studied extended over multiple generations as new family members learned the ways of their respective packs. They found that these idiosyncratic behaviors persisted because they conferred specific advantages to the group, enhancing their survival and cohesion.

Understanding Canine Culture

In the context of dogs, "culture" refers to the shared behaviors, practices, and social structures observed within a group of dogs. This culture encompasses various aspects such as:

- **Communication**: The ways dogs communicate with each other through body language, vocalizations, and scent marking.

- **Social Structure**: The hierarchy or social order within a pack, including roles such as leaders (alpha dogs) and followers.

- **Behavioral Norms**: Common behaviors and routines shared among the group, such as hunting techniques, play behaviors, and grooming practices.

- **Learning and Transmission**: How knowledge and behaviors are passed from generation to generation, often through observation and imitation.

For example, wild wolf packs exhibit complex social structures and cooperative behaviors that can be seen as cultural. Domesticated dogs also develop their own cultures within households or communities, adapting to human environments and social norms.

This culture, which includes territory preferences, hunting techniques, denning locations, and other social and behavioral subtleties, is a testament to the wolves' intricate social structure. Haber's observations of Denali National Park's wolves, particularly the Toklat wolves, revealed a behavioral repertoire that distinguished them among wolves. Their large and complex den site, mapped by Haber to exceed nearly five acres of warrens, tunnels, and various entrances and exits, is a marvel of nature.[40]

---

40   Among Wolves, Gordon Haber and Marybeth Holleman, University of Alaska Press ©2013

The Importance of Ritualization in Wolf Culture

The ritualization of behaviors within wolf packs is crucial for maintaining the social structure and cohesion of the group. These rituals help to establish and reinforce the roles and relationships within the pack, providing a sense of order and predictability. For wolves, this means that each member understands their place and responsibilities, reducing conflicts and promoting cooperation.

How I Leverage Culture to Facilitate My Work with Captive Wolves

Having worked with wolves directly for nearly 40 years, I have established a cultural dynamic that makes it easier for us to manage and care for our animals. We do this by encouraging specific repetitive behavioral patterns from when our animals are young and maintaining those patterns through adulthood, even as wolves move on and new animals join the family. Establishing and maintaining consistent patterns provide security and confidence and facilitate easier interactions with your animals.

Establishing Your Own Canine Culture

By establishing a canine culture, working with one or two animals, adding a third or a fourth becomes even easier because the original animals are indoctrinated into the culture, and the other animals are more inclined to follow their example. Establishing a culture isn't difficult. Simple things like regular feeding times, placement of bowls, which animals are fed first, how you travel in a vehicle, who you load first, how they're secured, and numerous other small details all add up to creating your own unique canine family culture.

The more consistent you are in applying your culture, the easier it is to maintain that dynamic in unfamiliar circumstances or when new animals join the group. Simple things like where we feed puppies, where puppies sleep, what time we feed, how we prepare to go on hikes, and who sleeps where in the house all amount to our unique culture. Currently, we have four generations of animals on the property, and it's fascinating to see how the strength of our culture has facilitated adding new animals without upsetting the order.

People have observed that what we've been able to accomplish is highly unusual. Most of the time, people working with captive wolves and high-content wolf dogs end up having to separate animals into male-female pairs to prevent conflicts from developing. While I can't say that we won't have to do that at some point in the future, at present, we have a 13-year-old animal, a 5-year-old animal, two females that are a year-and-a-half old, an 8-month-old malamute puppy, and a 5-and-a-half-month-old wolf puppy. The coexistence dynamic has been peaceful.

It's never easy to pinpoint the exact elements that allow such a harmonious situation to persist. However, I attribute much of our success to the consistent ritualization of many aspects of our day-to-day lives. Our animals know what to expect from me and my wife and from each other, reducing anxiety and minimizing unpredictable behaviors, such as aggression towards one another.

Every family has its own culture, including families comprised of multiple species. Your family culture includes how you communicate, the social structure of your family, what you do and how you act collectively (behavioral norms), and how you learn, share, and apply new information.

No two families are the same.

So, what's the Wolfy Wisdom? Simple. Find a rhythm. Identify things that you can repeat and repeat them every single day. Indoctrinate your animals into your way of life and don't mix it up without good reason. As you add new animals to the family group, remember how important it is to adhere to the "original dog first" principle. Your mature and experienced canine companions will help set the stage for newcomers, and by leveraging their experience and the rituals you've established with them, you'll find you'll vastly simplify your multiple-dog household living and working arrangements.

Jake (with the light eyes) and Jessa, just minutes before my mistake precipitated an attack.

Chapter 20:

When Things Go Wrong

The Day My Wolf Ate Me

Sometimes, no matter how hard you try to avoid it, things can go sideways for you, but probably not nearly as spectacularly as they did on me in January of 1992. At the time, I was living in the Colorado Rockies, high above Boulder, Colorado. On the day of the incident, it was minus 20 degrees, and I was dressed for the weather. It's a good thing, too, because if I'd been wearing any less clothing, I might have lost my arms.

I was out with the first wild wolf I'd ever had, Jake, the one Colorado Parks and Wildlife remanded to my care on the advice of one of my professors. Along with Jake, I had Jessa, a female wolfdog I'd had from the moment she was born. And aiding me on the day was my then-girlfriend, Leah. Leah was a feisty calf roper, who grew up on her family's ranch and subsequently attended Cal-Poly on a rodeo scholarship. Others described Leah as a "firecracker." She described herself as a 6'2" woman crammed into a 5'2" body. I called her Frankie —a nickname I gave her as she was a combination of feisty and cranky. We'd been shooting photos for a wildlife magazine when we realized we had begun to lose the light, and it became imperative that we get off the mountain.

Losing My Patience Was My First Mistake

At the time, we were roughly two miles up a snow-packed, single-track trail, with our vehicle parked along the roadway down below. I'd already put Jake back on a leash, but I had a problem with Jessa. She loved playing keep-away, and I was cold and losing my patience. Allowing myself to become frustrated was my first mistake. When working with wolves, you'd better have inexhaustible patience, or you're asking for trouble. Every time I'd try to grab Jessa, she'd leap beyond my reach, and I grew progressively more irritated with every missed attempt.

Late winter is breeding season for wolves, and because wolves only breed once a year, it's a particularly serious business. Male wolves, in particular, can get prickly at this time, and if I'd been more experienced, I would have realized that I was setting myself up for a problem based on how Jake was reacting to my efforts to corral his little girlfriend.

Finally, Jessa shot between my legs, and I pounced, grabbing her by the scruff to get her under control. Unfortunately, Jake perceived what I did to Jessa as aggression, and he had had enough. I had my right hand around Jessa's scruff, which, unfortunately, was right in front of Jake's face, and he didn't hesitate.

The Fight of My Life

With a bone-crunching snap of his jaws, he grabbed hold of my forearm and immediately pulverized both bones. So fast and explosive was his attack that, for a moment, my brain couldn't process what was happening. It almost felt like I'd been struck by lightning. But Jake wasn't done with me by a long shot. The moment I realized I was in trouble, I attempted to regain control of the situation by throwing myself on top of Jake and trying to wrap the arm that wasn't in his mouth around his neck to get him off his feet. Although the incident probably lasted between 45 and 90 seconds, it felt like an eternity, and my consciousness seemed to have splintered into three distinct roles.

In one, I was in a life-or-death fight for my life, rolling on the ground and wrestling with this viciously attacking wolf. The other was like a drone five feet above the ground, surveying the event with a cool and unbiased eye. And the third splinter of consciousness was the dispassionate scientist calmly speaking to me. The first thing he said was, "Wow, he's a lot stronger than you expected, isn't he?" As the attack persisted, I could feel bones, tendons, and everything else in my arm splintering and giving way.

In a desperate effort to relieve the pressure, I stuffed my fully gloved left hand into his mouth. Despite my forearm being fully within his jaws, he bit down harder and managed to fracture all four of my fingers transversely. Meanwhile, Leah was screaming, "What do I do? What do I do?" I'm not sure which version of my consciousness shouted the instructions, but from somewhere came "grab him by the nuts." Only an insane and fearless woman would have leaped into such a fray and grabbed a wolf by the balls. But that's what Leah did. Suddenly, the pressure was gone. I staggered backward, attempting to get to my feet and get away from Jake, but he wasn't ready to relent.

I'm alive today to tell the story because Leah was a fast, fearless, and supremely athletic horsewoman. She did what she claimed any ranch chick would do, which was the one thing required to save my life. She grabbed a hold of the loose end of Jake's leash.

He hurled himself towards my face and throat to put me down once and for all. But because Leah had wrapped the end of the rope around a tree branch at lightning speed, he came up short with his front teeth finding purchase, not in my throat, but in my left bicep. It felt like a rubber band exploding in my arm. Immediately, I lost all sensation in my already broken hand. Fortunately, Jake's aggression was only directed towards me, and he didn't turn on Leah.

"I'm Going to Get a Gun and Shoot Him. He's Too Dangerous."

As I cradled my mangled arms to my chest, the scientist version of my consciousness was coolly informing me that I was **hemorrhaging** and badly hurt and that I probably had less than 45 minutes to get somewhere safe and warm, or I was unlikely to leave the mountain. Meanwhile, Leah was screaming, "I've got to get a gun and shoot Jake. He's too dangerous." But I didn't have time for that argument, and I had no intention of letting anyone kill an animal because I'd messed up. In spite of the severity of my injuries, I bore Jake no malice and had no intention of allowing him to come to harm on account of me. I calmly said to Leah, "I'm badly hurt, and I don't know how much time I've got left. Give me a five-minute head start, then bring Jessa and Jake down the trail and meet me at the truck. You'll either find me there or laid out along the trail." I didn't have time to argue further, and I turned and began stumbling towards the road below.

My memory of the two miles off the hill was fractured and hazy. I couldn't feel either of my arms and held them to my chest. Between my injuries and adrenaline, I kept stumbling and falling, and every time I did, I had to crawl to my feet without the use of my arms. Finally, after what seemed like a hundred years, I could see the icy ribbon of asphalt and the truck below. But when I got to the vehicle, I had a whole new problem. I couldn't open it. I didn't have the use of my hands. I stood there, shivering in the cold, waiting for Leah to make her way back with the wolves. When she did, I told her she'd have to load them up before I could get in the vehicle. Luckily, she was able to manage the task.

She insisted we immediately head to the local emergency room, but I told her we couldn't do that and that we had to get the animals back in the habitat first. I couldn't afford for the authorities to get involved with this incident, which could result in me losing my animals. By this time, Leah was willing to do what I instructed, and we took the animals home before finally making our way to the emergency room at Boulder's Community Hospital.

On arrival at the ER, the trauma experts cut away my clothes. I was shocked to see that I did not have any open wounds, but my right forearm looked like a bag filled with blood, and my left hand looked like a boxing glove without the glove.

After examining my injuries and doing an x-ray, the on-call surgeon told me they were going to try to save my arm below the elbow. At first, I didn't register what they were saying, but finally, I realized they were discussing an **amputation**. I didn't like this idea, and even though I was now hopped up on a massive dose of morphine and still in various stages of shock due to my injuries, I insisted that this was not the outcome I would accept. I begged Leah to drive me to Vail and the Steadman-Hawkins Clinic with the idea that if anyone could save my arm and hand, it was that team.

Did I mention I didn't have insurance? The team at Boulder's Hospital was not optimistic about my prospects, but I didn't really give them a choice. They shot me up with more morphine, and Leah drove me through the night to the clinic in Vail. I must have passed out because I don't remember the drive or sitting in the parking lot waiting for doctors to show up there.

Later, I learned that Leah had explained the situation to the Stedman-Hawkins team. Perhaps because of their curiosity as well as their kind-heartedness, they agreed to work on me pro bono. It turned out I had over 37 fully displaced fractures in my right arm, four complete transverse breaks in my left hand, ruptured muscle **sheaths** and tendons in my right forearm, and an 80% tear of my left bicep.

I was one of the first people in the country to have an **external fixator** to place the displaced bones in their proper positions and hold them where they were supposed to be while they could mend. I had four pins inserted from my first to my second knuckle to support the transverse fractures in my left hand, and they could do nothing for the partially ruptured bicep but hope that it healed. I was lucky. My inexperience and lack of focus on the right thing at the right time nearly cost me my life, and if I hadn't had a fierce and competent partner, there's no way I would have made it off the mountain alive.

In the years since this experience, I've had many full-grown male wolves during the breeding season, yet I never encountered behavior so extreme as what Jake exhibited. I credit the attack to several factors. The main one was my inexperience. But also, even though I had spent a ton of time with Jake, I didn't raise him from a young puppy, and it's possible that in his mind, I was never family in the way I am to any other animal I've had.

What Happened to Jake?

Many people ask me, what happened to Jake? After all, he was just being a wolf, and I was the one who screwed up. I'm happy to report that even though I could no longer keep that animal, I was fortunate to find alternate accommodations that allowed him to have a nice, long, comfortable life in a biologically appropriate habitat with a beautiful wolf partner named Indigo. The owner of the other facility and I agreed to collaborate, and Jake was allowed to breed with Indigo, producing a litter from which I got a single male pup I named Tahoe. A second, different pairing resulted in another female named Karma, and those wolves went on to help me educate thousands of people over more than a decade.

How to Avoid Ending Up in Similar Situation

Hopefully, you'll never experience anything remotely approximating what I went through with my mistake, but even the most minor attack by an aggressive canine can be a traumatizing experience. The first goal, of course, is to avoid such an experience altogether. Your first goal to avoid having things go wrong is to be patient with your animals. Observing their behavior should give you a very good idea of their emotional state. Dogs that are preparing to attack you don't make a secret of it. They are not **ambush predators**, particularly with domestic dogs; their inclination is only to attack as a last resort. They'll give you many signals first, telling you that you're crossing boundaries that you shouldn't cross, and only when you've pushed them over any reasonable threshold will they resort to causing their human physical harm.

Some of the more obvious ones are ear position—are the ears pulled flat back against the skull? Wolf handlers call this appearance "airplane ears be-cause the ears have the swept-back appearance of fighter jet wings, nar-rowed eyes, tight lips, exposed teeth, possibly a sticking-out tongue, and a tail that is either tucked tightly under the belly or worse, extended straight out in a position I call "kill-o-clock" that indicates an aggressive threat be-havior.

Defending Yourself

Of course, sometimes the animal inclined to attack you is not yours and is one with which you're unfamiliar. In this case, it may be more challenging to determine what is provoking the behavior. Typically, backing away while focusing on the aggressive dog is enough to offset an attack.

In the wild or in containment, when people feel threatened by wolves, the appropriate actions are simple and straightforward. Don't turn your back on the animal. Never run. Stay upright, and if possible, raise your hands and any jacket you have above your head to make yourself look even larger. Because humans always stand on their hind legs, we already look big and aggressive to canines, and typically, a confident and calm retreat is sufficient to avoid any impending attack. But if a dog continues to become aggressive, the best thing you can do is unleash your inner grizzly bear. Roar, scream, growl, widen your eyes, and look like an even fiercer predator than the dog. Most canines with aggressive tendencies are not used to humans that return the favor. If you have something you can use to make noise or defend yourself, all the better. I particularly like metal trash cans held as shields and banged as gongs. That combination puts the fear of God or humans in almost every canine I've ever seen. Having something like a trash can wielded as a shield is an excellent defense if, despite everything, a dog insists on attacking.

De-Escalating Fighting Dogs

The other place where things sometimes go wrong is when canines attack one another. Professional wolf handlers live with this possibility because captive wolves can get mad at each other and resolve their differences with severe aggression.

Facilities like mine employ **bite boxes** containing several tools to divert an attack, gain control of attacking animals, and prevent them from harming their handlers or each other. Surprisingly, our first weapon of choice is simply cheap perfume. As I mentioned in a prior chapter, canines are largely **olfactorily** driven. A sudden blast of a powerful odorant is sufficiently disorienting that many times, a couple of blasts of perfume betwixt two conflicting canines is sufficient to stop the attack and provide handlers the brief opportunity to regain control of the situation.

We also use **bite sticks**, a device like a broom handle with duct tape or even a tether at one end so the handler can maintain their grip, with the idea that if the animals are biting anything, you can give them something that isn't you or another wolf. Finally, we use a tool called a y-Pole for facilities with particularly challenging animals or animals that can't be handled for medical care or other interventions. I'll put a picture of one and a description below in case you're interested to see what those look like.

So what's the Wolfy Wisdom with preventing things from going wrong? First and foremost, don't push it. Every being has its limits, and it's better not to cross your dog's. Pay attention to body language. Dogs are visual communicators. Their expressions, how they hold their tail, the way their ears are pointed, whether their lips are curled back exposing the teeth, and of course, any guttural vocalizations should be cues that you're pressing it and should take a step back.

Many times, all you need to do is give an animal space, and the situation will attenuate. Should things go wrong, remain calm. Back away while facing the animal and do not run. The worst thing that can happen if one or more dogs are attacking you is for you to attempt to run away, fall, and let the dogs attack you while you're down. It's critical to always retain your composure, even if you're terrified.

Dogs know when they've got the upper hand, and if they're already inclined to be aggressive, they're going to exploit it. Bear in mind that domestic dogs and even wolves tend to be good-natured animals who don't routinely fight with each other, except when there's no other alternative. Just keep your **wits** about you, and you'll probably never find yourself receiving an actual, **uninhibited** attack.

A final thought here—you're more likely to witness dog-on-dog conflict than dog-on-human conflict. It can be hazardous to attempt to separate two fighting dogs, especially if you're alone. While with two people, each person can grab the hind legs of an attacking dog and "wheelbarrow" them apart. But keep in mind you're putting yourself at risk of the dog turning around and attacking you. This is why professionals have tools at their disposal including perfume, hoses, bite-sticks, and y-poles.

As with all things dog-related, paying attention to your dog, and anticipating rather than reacting will serve you well and help you maintain calm, Sharpener-like control of the situation.

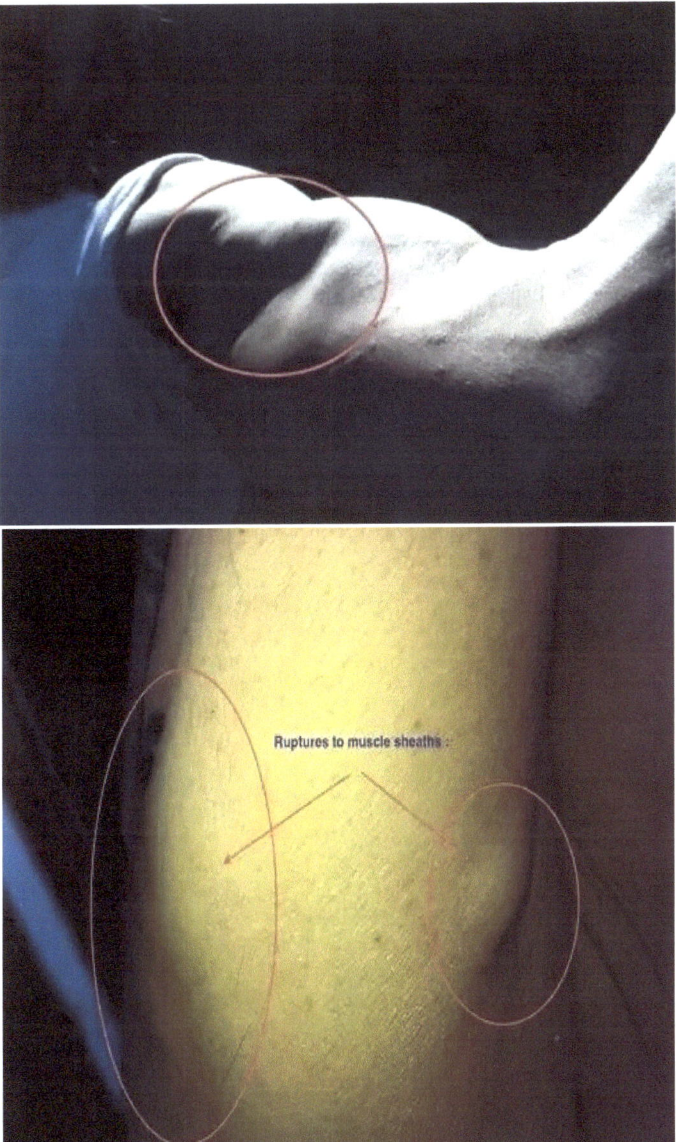

My injuries 20 years after the attack.

Chapter 21:

Final Thoughts

As you reach the conclusion of this book, I trust that you've found it as enlightening to read as it was for me to write. It's been a privilege to share my unique experiences with wolves, my deep understanding of their wild behaviors, and my insights on how these can be harnessed to enrich your life with your domestic canine companions. I'm confident that this work has fulfilled its promise to revolutionize your relationship with dogs.

And I hope, above all, that armed with your newfound knowledge, you develop a deeper appreciation for wolves and the wolf within your dog. By applying the practical insights from this book, you will be well-equipped to unravel the reasons behind many of the behaviors your dog displays each day. Your greater understanding will enable you to adapt your lifestyle to foster the best, most harmonious, and happiest relationships with the dogs that share your life.

If you are interested in supporting my work in the future, you can buy my children's book, *The Little Malamute Raised by Wolves*. You can also support my nonprofit, the Tahoe Wolf Center, and its goal to foster a greater understanding of wild wolves and to support new and improved coexistence strategies to help people struggling to deal with wolves in the areas where they are recovering.

Finally, my nonprofit is committed to reshaping the legislative landscape concerning wolves nationally and globally. I aspire for wolves to be protected and allowed to thrive in all suitable habitats worldwide. If you wish to support other causes of wolf conservation, I've compiled a list in the appendix of this book. I've also included a list of additional readings for those who want to deepen their understanding of wolves and canine behavior.

If you would like to work with me directly on habitat design or dietary strategies, you can contact me via my nonprofit and schedule a consultation. If you'd like to keep track of my work with the wolves in my household, you can follow me on YouTube, Twitter, Instagram, and TikTok. I will also launch a Substack where you can subscribe to a community of like-minded people who wish to learn more about wolves, work with their dogs, and share ideas to improve canines' lives.

From the bottom of my heart, thank you for reading this work. I hope you look back on the experience and smile at how much you've learned and how much better your life with dogs has become.

~ Oliver "The Wolf Guy" Starr

"The bond with a true dog is as lasting as the ties of this earth will ever be." — Konrad Lorenz

Epilogue:

Wolves Are in Peril

Wolves Are in Peril

Today, wolves are in more peril than they've been at any time since 1975, when President Nixon enacted the Endangered Species Act, granting wolves full protections across the entire lower 48 U.S. states. At the time, wolves had been entirely extirpated from every part of this country except for the far north woods in Minnesota. Because of the protections enacted under the Endangered Species Act, and as a consequence of the successful reintroduction effort in Yellowstone National Park and Idaho, today there are roughly 10,000 wolves in the lower 48, with the largest populations being in Minnesota, Wisconsin, Idaho, Montana, Wyoming, Oregon, Washington, and California.

Wolves: When Politics Trump Science

However, due to recent congressional legislative actions, wolves have lost much of their protection in the places where they are recovering. Presently, Idaho has a plan to kill off 90 percent of its wolf population. Montana isn't far behind, and just this week, the Wyoming legislature voted to make it legal to run over wolves and coyotes with snowmobiles as a means of fair chase. Currently, an act deceptively called the "Trust the Science Act" just passed Congress in what is the latest effort to use legislation, rather than science, to remove Endangered Species Act protections from wolves across the US, granting broad management authority to the states. Should this premature and unscientific delisting pass, wolf recovery will be truncated to the point populations will never recover across a meaningful portion of wolves' prior range.

The reasons for this are multifold. Ranchers and extractive industry, including logging, mining, and hunting, are deeply entrenched in the political power structure in the United States and most strongly in the American West. These groups have literally been making the rules as they go for the last 200 years, and unless we vote them, and the politicians beholden to their interests out, their influence will persist to the detriment of our public lands and all the wild creatures that rely on our vanishing vast open spaces to survive. If you wish to learn more about this particular topic, please read the astonishing but horrifying book, *This Land: How Cowboys, Capitalism, and Corruption are Ruining the American West by Christopher Ketcham*.[41]

Unfortunately, with the exception of California, where wolves are on the state's endangered species protection list, the likelihood is that if states are granted management rights, wolf protections will be dismantled entirely, and wolf recovery will wink out.

A Plague That Only Wolves Can Curb

People who bought this book because they love wolves already know that wolves play a critical role in maintaining healthy ecosystems, that they are not a threat to people, and that their impact on livestock and big game herds is not only negligible but also critical in keeping elk and deer populations healthy and vibrant. The positive effect of wolves is more crucial today than ever.

---

41   https://www.amazon.com/This-Land-Christopher-Ketcham-audiobook/dp/B07TVKWLGM/ref=sr_1_4?sr=8-4

Over the last 60 years, an unstoppable plague has been assaulting elk and deer populations throughout the United States. Correctly known as chronic wasting disease[42], this plague has also been called zombie deer disease. It is an infection of the brain caused by a misfolded protein known as a prion. In humans, a variant of this disease is known as Creutzfeldt-Jakob, and it is always fatal after an incubation period of up to 20 years.

Interestingly, recently published scientific studies have found that wolves can identify this disease far before it is symptomatic in game populations, and they selectively prey on infected animals since they're easier to hunt and kill. As a result, we see marked differences in the prevalence of this disease in areas with robust wolf populations and a significant increase in the presence of this disease in others. Wisconsin is a perfect example, where counties with a substantial wolf population have tested incidents of chronic wasting disease of under 26%, whereas counties lacking wolves have an incidence upwards of 74%.

Infected animals are not safe to eat, and recently, two hunters who are known to have consumed deer meat from an area where the disease is endemic were both identified post-mortem as having contracted Creutzfeldt-Jakob. In other words, this disease has apparently managed to cross from wild **ungulate** populations to humans. This prospect is terrifying since the disease is not symptomatic for many years and potentially spreads without anybody knowing it. Worse, infected animals leave infectious material in their droppings, which are then transmitted to grasses and consumed by other ungulates, creating a vicious cycle of infection and reinfection.

Scientists concur that it is only a matter of time before livestock grazing in impacted areas also becomes victim to this unstoppable disease that has no cure or means of reducing the incidence or severity aside from predation.

The entire livestock industry will face an existential threat when this disease jumps into livestock. Several decades ago, a variant of this disease became present in Scottish and British sheep populations, and they killed millions of animals in an effort to curtail the infection.[43]

---

42   https://www.sciencedirect.com/science/article/pii/S2405844024079829
43   https://www.centerforfoodsafety.org/issues/1040/mad-cow-disease/timeline-mad-cow-disease-outbreaks

Because of the extremely long incubation period, it could be years before this disease is detected in domestic cattle populations, which means humans could have been unknowingly infected for decades. If this doesn't terrify you, I don't know what would.

Based on this information, ranchers and hunters would likely favor strong wolf protections and robust wolf populations to help reduce the incidence of this disease and control it before it turns from a smolder to a conflagration.

Alas, they don't seem to understand just how dangerous this situation is, and they routinely spread misinformation in a misguided effort to encourage the removal of wolf populations from everywhere they persist.

Colorado's Wolf Reintroduction

In what some saw as a bright spot in the general dismal news for wolves, a first-of-its-kind ballot initiative in Colorado mandated the reintroduction of wolves to the state no later than December 31st, 2023.

Unfortunately, the effort has resulted in more acrimony than positivity. The initiative barely passed with a razor-thin margin of less than half a percent,[44] representing a near-perfect split between rural communities, which were nearly uniformly opposed, and urban areas, which were proponents.

Given CWD's existential threat to the livestock industry, you'd think that ranchers would be among the first to advocate for wolves' recovery. Alas, this is not the case, and the outcry from the cattle associations has been sustained and plaintive despite the paltry number of wolves, their negligible impact on cattle, and the incalculable ecological and financial value a recovered Colorado wolf population represents.

Ultimately, eleven wolves were released in a state of 66.3 million acres, of which 24 million acres are classified as public lands. Colorado has approximately 2.61 million cattle, including 643,000 beef cows and 197,000 milk cows. Additionally, the state has about 400,000 sheep and lambs (National Agricultural Statistics Service).

---

44   https://www.smithsonianmag.com/smart-news/colorado-will-reintroduce-endangered-gray-wolves-this-month-180983375/

In other words, there are over 273,000 head of livestock for each wolf in the state. A number so small that as a percent, it's expressed as 0.000365%.

Nevertheless, the Colorado ranching community has gone insane over a dozen wolves in their presence. So insane, in fact, that when the first pack in Colorado in over a hundred years to have offspring killed a few cattle, ranchers forced the state to capture the animals and put them in captivity.

As a result, the breeding male was killed, and state agents are still trying to track and capture one pup that went unaccounted for to reunite it with its captured family before it dies of starvation. Between the ranchers and the state's botched efforts to handle the situation, what should have been a beautiful environmental success story has become a public relations and biological disaster, all because a few recalcitrant producers, largely grazing livestock on public lands, made a stink about a dozen big wild dogs.

My Mission

I'm telling you this because I believe that the only way we will ever see sustainable wolf recovery in the United States is if people at large care about wolves and demand that they're treated reasonably and given the federal protections they deserve so they can enact their critical ecosystem management roles in numbers large enough to be meaningful.

Beyond my goal to help showcase the remarkable and complex behaviors of wolves, elucidate how closely your dogs mirror so many of them, and, by leveraging this knowledge, help you achieve an even better and more fulfilling relationship with your canine family members, this book exists to help support my lifetime objective to change the prospects for wolves worldwide.

To do this, I need to put a million people in front of wolves before I'm too old to do the work. I believe the best way to accomplish this goal is through the Tahoe Wolf Center, a science-based education and advocacy organization in the South Lake Tahoe area. My objective is to purchase and rewild an unsuccessful golf course and place on the landscape in a 25-acre habitat a captive family group of wolves that can be observed through an indoor viewing auditorium through one-way glass and closed-circuit television, allowing the public to get a glimpse of actual social dynamics and beautiful behaviors of this iconic species.

If you love wolves and believe that they should be treated equitably, and if you love the wolf in your dog and want to understand your canine family member better, please buy this book not just for yourself but for friends and family members who will appreciate what's here. Not only will you be doing yourself and your canine companions a favor, but you will also be helping me in my mission to make sure that wolves exist on the landscape for your children, their children, and children a hundred years from now.

If you wish to support my efforts, there are several things you can do. You can make tax-deductible donations to my nonprofit, the Tahoe Wolf Center, a federally registered 501(c)3 - tax exempt organization, you can buy an extra copy of this book and give it to someone you know who loves wolves, you can subscribe to a membership plan on my YouTube Channel: https://www.youtube.com/@OliverTheWolfGuy, buy my other books, including my children's book, *The Little Malamute Raised by Wolves*, and, of course, you can spread the word about my project and the plight of wolves in general.

For those that wish to get in touch with me for consulting, large grants or gifts, or with offers to collaborate, please email me: Inquiries@tahoewolfcenter.com

If you want to see what else we're up to, you can follow us on the social media accounts below:

@owstarr - X
@tahoewolfcenter - X
@ostarr - Instagram
@thewolves.bsky.social
LinkedIn
@ostarr - Threads.net
https://mas.to/@owstarr
@oliverthewolfguy - TikTok

Author's Note

A word about the terminology used in this book: in writing this book, I have frequently used the terms "wolf" and "wolfdog" interchangeably. Generally speaking, when referring to my animals, I often use the term "wolves." However, all the animals under my care are wolf ambassadors, except Jake, whom I received directly from Colorado Parks and Wildlife decades ago. My animals, not explicitly referred to as Alaskan Malamutes, are high-content wolfdog ambassadors.

These animals are indistinguishable visibly and behaviorally from their wild cousins for all practical purposes. However, they are not pure wolves extracted from the wild. The reason I've chosen to refer to them as wolves is simply out of convenience and because their behavior and appearance are analogous to wolves. It avoids the confusion of having to consistently explain what the differences are. From a practical standpoint, high-content wolfdogs are those animals that are visibly indistinguishable from wolves, even to experts, and whose genetic testing reveals at least 95% genetic matches to known wolf DNA. All of the animals referenced in this work align with this standard.

Glossary

- **Adrenaline:** A hormone released in response to stress or excitement, increasing heart rate and energy.

- **Ambush Predator:** A predator that relies on stealth to catch prey rather than pursuing it.

- **Amputation:** The surgical removal of a limb or body part.

- **Bite Box:** A tool used by animal handlers to prevent aggressive behavior by providing an object for animals to bite.

- **Bite Stick:** A device designed to divert an attacking animal's attention, it is often used in animal handling.

- **Cohesion:** The action or fact of forming a united whole, often used to describe group behavior in social animals.

- **Deferential:** Showing respectful submission or yielding to the judgment or opinion of others.

- **Disperser:** Also known as lone wolves, dispersers are wolves who have left their natal (family) group to seek out an opposite-sex wolf and territory with adequate prey populations that is not already occupied by other wolves.

- **Domestication:** The process by which wild animals or plants have been adapted to live alongside humans, often resulting in significant changes to their behavior, morphology, and genetics.

- **Embodied:** To be given a physical form or presence; to represent something in a tangible way.

- ♣ **Emotional Intelligence:** The ability to recognize, understand, and manage one's own emotions as well as the emotions of others.

- ♣ **Ethology:** The scientific study of animal behavior in natural conditions.

- ♣ **External Fixator:** A medical device used to stabilize fractured bones from the outside of the body.

- ♣ **Ferocious:** Extremely aggressive or violent.

- ♣ **Guttural:** A sound produced in the throat; harsh or throaty.

- ♣ **Hemorrhaging:** Losing a large amount of blood in a short period.

- ♣ **Human-Centric:** A viewpoint that places humans at the center of consideration, often disregarding the rights or needs of non-human entities.

- ♣ **Interspecies Communication:** Interaction and information exchange between different species.

- ♣ **Intrinsically:** In a way that is essential or inherent to something.

- ♣ **Olfactorily:** Related to the sense of smell.

- ♣ **Oxytocin:** Oxytocin is a hormone and neurotransmitter often referred to as the "love hormone" or "bonding hormone." It plays a crucial role in social bonding, emotional regulation, and reproductive behaviors, such as childbirth and breastfeeding. Oxytocin levels increase during positive social interactions, including physical touch, and are associated with feelings of affection, trust, and empathy.

Research has shown that spending time physically close to dogs can increase oxytocin levels in both humans and dogs. When humans pet or cuddle with dogs, oxytocin is released in humans and dogs, fostering a mutual bond. This effect has been widely documented in studies showing that interactions with dogs can lower stress and increase feelings of well-being.

While most studies on oxytocin and bonding have focused on domesticated animals like dogs, the same hormone could also be involved in interactions between humans and wolves, particularly those raised in controlled environments or with regular exposure to humans. Wolves are known for their strong social bonds within their packs and with humans they trust. Although the effects may be more complex due to the wild nature of wolves, positive physical interactions with wolves could also stimulate oxytocin release in both humans and wolves. However, more research is needed to fully understand the dynamics of oxytocin in human-wolf interactions, especially outside of domesticated settings.

- **Raw-Dog:** A term referring to wolves or dogs in their true natural form, unvarnished by the selective breeding efforts of humans. Wolves are considered raw dogs, possessing all their instincts and behaviors undiluted by ***domestication***.

- **Sheaths:** Protective coverings or casings, often referring to muscles or tendons in a biological context.

- **Social Cohesion:** The bonds that unite members of a social group, facilitating cooperation and collective action.

- **Tactile:** Related to the sense of touch.

- **Transverse Break**: A fracture that runs perpendicular to the bone's length.

- **Trauma:** A severe injury or shock to the body.

- **Ungulate:** A member of a diverse group of large mammals that includes horses, cattle, deer, and giraffes, characterized by having hooves.

- **Umwelt:** A term in biology referring to the subjective world experienced by an organism; the way an animal perceives its environment.

- **Uninhibited:** Not restrained or suppressed.

- **Vital:** Necessary or important; essential.

- **Wits:** The ability to think and make decisions quickly; intelligence.

- **Y-Pole:** A tool used in animal handling that allows handlers to safely manage aggressive animals.

Additional Resources

Books:

1. ***A Wolf of My Own*** - The book that inspired my lifelong passion for wolves by Jan Wahl, illustrated by Lillian Hoban.

2. ***Among Wolves: Insights into Alaska's Most Misunderstood Predator*** by Gordon Haber and Marybeth Holleman
   - Purchase Link: https://a.co/d/5E1VmqL

3. ***Canine Enrichment for the Real World: Making It a Part of Your Dog's Daily Life*** by Allie Bender and Emily Strong
   - Purchase Link: https://a.co/d/7iDj74S

4. ***Doggie Body Language: A Dog Lover's Guide to Understanding Your Best Friend*** by Lili Chin
   - Purchase Link: https://a.co/d/hto6jnJ

5. ***Give Your Dog a Bone*** by Ian Billinghurst
   - Purchase Link: https://a.co/d/1Fgxtmb

6. ***Inside of a Dog: What Dogs See, Smell, and Know*** by Alexandra Horowitz
   - Purchase Link: https://www.simonandschuster.com/books/Inside-of-a-Dog/Alexandra-Horowitz/9781416583431

7. ***Our Oldest Companions*** by Pat Shipman
   - Purchase Link: https://a.co/d/2uNNwvA

8. ***The Forever Dog: Surprising New Science to Help Your Canine Companion Live Younger, Healthier, and Longer*** by Rodney Habib and Karen Shaw Becker
   - 🐾 Purchase Link:https://www.harpercollins.com/products/the-forever-dog-rodney-habibkaren-shaw-becker?variant=40989649571810

9. ***The Genius of Dogs: How Dogs Are Smarter Than You Think*** by Brian Hare and Vanessa Woods
   - 🐾 Purchase Link: https://a.co/d/j0dg6RJ

10. ***The Invaders*** by Pat Shipman
    - 🐾 Purchase Link: https://a.co/d/7KSji3B

11. ***Wolves: Behavior, Ecology, and Conservation*** by L. David Mech and Luigi Boitano
    - 🐾 Purchase Link: https://a.co/d/bHDcT7e

12. ***Wolfdogs A to Z*** by Nicole Wilde
    - 🐾 Purchase Link: https://a.co/d/4re9Vrq

13. ***This Land: How Cowboys, Capitalism, and Corruption are Ruining the American West*** by Christopher Ketcham (Paperback)
    - 🐾 Purchase Link: https://a.co/d/foZL4zq

14. **Wolfer** - The first-person story of bringing wolves back to Yellowstone National Park by Carter Niemeyer
    - 🐾 Purchase Link: https://a.co/d/eMWk3aF

15. **Dog Language** - An Encyclopedia of Canine Behavior by Roger Abrantes
    - 🐾 Purchase Link: https://www.amazon.com/Dog-Language-Encyclopedia-Canine-Behavior/dp/0966048407?utm_source=chatgpt.com

Products:

1. **Fi Tracking Collars:**
   - 🐾 Description: GPS tracking collars for dogs to monitor their location and activity.
   - 🐾 Purchase Link: https://tryfi.com/

2. **Outdoor Dog Supply Collars:**
   - Description: Durable collars designed for active outdoor dogs, offering comfort and performance.
   - Purchase Link: https://www.outdoordogsupply.com

3. **Real Meat Dog Food:**
   - Description: A premium, grain-free, and raw-inspired dog food made with real meat.
   - Purchase Link: https://www.realmeatpet.com/foods.html

4. **Topples**:
   - Description: Durable treat-dispensing dog toys.
   - Purchase Link: https://westpaw.com/products/toppl-treat-toy

5. **Y-Poles:**
   - Description: Used for safely separating animals.
   - Purchase Link: https://freemanbydesign.com/freeman-y-pole/

6. **ZiwiPeak:**
   - Description: A high-quality, natural dog food that focuses on whole prey ingredients.
   - Purchase Link: https://us.ziwipets.com/

7. **PetSpan** – Canine Longevity Programs
   - Purchase Link: https://www.petspan.com/

8. **Impact Dog Crates**: the safest, most secure, and highest quality dog training crates on Earth (it's what we use).
   - Purchase Link: https://www.impactdogcrates.com/

9. **Learn More about Wolves in the Wolves Masterclass by Professor Marco Adda**
   - Purchase Link: https://www.marcoadda.com/wolves-online-masterclass

10. **Organic Wool Dryer Balls: Woolsies**
    - Purchase Link: https://a.co/d/4l81dk6

Conservation and Rescue Organizations

1. **Animal Wellness Action**
    - https://www.animalwellnessaction.org
    - Advocates for policies to prevent animal cruelty and promote wildlife conservation, including protections for wolves and other keystone species.

2. **Center for Biological Diversity**
    - https://www.biologicaldiversity.org
    - Combines science, law, and activism to protect endangered species and their habitats, including wolves and other keystone species.

3. **Defenders of Wildlife**
    - https://www.defenders.org
    - Works to protect and restore imperiled species and their habitats throughout North America, with a significant focus on wolves.

4. **EarthJustice**
    - https://earthjustice.org
    - A nonprofit environmental law organization that uses legal action to protect wildlife, combat climate change, and advance clean energy.

5. **Grand Canyon Wolf Recovery Project**
    - https://www.gcwolfrecovery.org
    - Works to recover and protect wolves in the Grand Canyon region through education, science, and advocacy.

6. **International Wolf Center**
    - https://www.wolf.org
    - Advances the survival of wolf populations by teaching about wolves and their relationship to wildlands.

7. **Living With Wolves**
    - https://www.livingwithwolves.org
    - Educates the public about wolves and their role in maintaining healthy ecosystems through science-based information.

8. **Mission: Wolf**
    - https://www.missionwolf.org

♣ A sanctuary providing a safe home for captive wolves and wolfdogs while educating the public about these misunderstood animals.

9. National Wolfwatcher Coalition
♣ https://wolfwatcher.org
♣ Advocates for the protection of wolf populations across the United States through education and advocacy.

10. Predator Defense
♣ https://www.predatordefense.org
♣ A nonprofit dedicated to protecting native predators and ending inhumane wildlife management practices.

11. Project Coyote
♣ https://www.projectcoyote.org
♣ Promotes coexistence between people and wildlife through education, science, and advocacy, with a focus on native carnivores.

12. ROAM Wolf Sanctuary
♣ https://www.roamwithus.org
♣ A sanctuary dedicated to providing a safe environment for rescued wolves and wolfdogs, focusing on their care and well-being.

13. Tahoe Wolf Center
♣ https://www.tahoewolfcenter.org
♣ Dedicated to wolf conservation and education through research, advocacy, and educational programs.

14. The Rewilding Institute
♣ https://rewilding.org
♣ Focused on restoring and protecting large wildlands and reintroducing species to rewild ecosystems.

15. Western Watersheds Project
♣ https://www.westernwatersheds.org
♣ Works to protect and restore western watersheds and wildlife, with efforts to reduce livestock grazing on public lands.

16. Wild Spirit Wolf Sanctuary
♣ https://www.wildspiritwolfsanctuary.org
♣ Provides sanctuary for wolves and wolfdogs, educating the public

about wild canids and their care.

17. WildEarth Guardians
- https://www.wildearthguardians.org
- Protects and restores the wildlife, wild places, and wild rivers of the American West through advocacy and legal action.

18. Wildlands Defense
- https://wildlandsdefense.org
- Dedicated to defending wild places and wildlife in the western United States from industrial development and habitat destruction.

19. Wildlife Coexistence Network
- https://www.wildlifecoexistence.org
- Focuses on creating solutions for peaceful coexistence between humans and wildlife, especially predators.

20. Yamnuska Wolfdog Sanctuary
- https://www.yamnuskawolfdogsanctuary.com
- A sanctuary for wolfdogs that educates the public about their unique needs and helps rescue and rehome these animals.

21. Wolf Conservation Center
- https://nywolf.org
- Promotes wolf conservation through education, advocacy, and participation in species recovery programs.